# Fifteen Days in Urgain

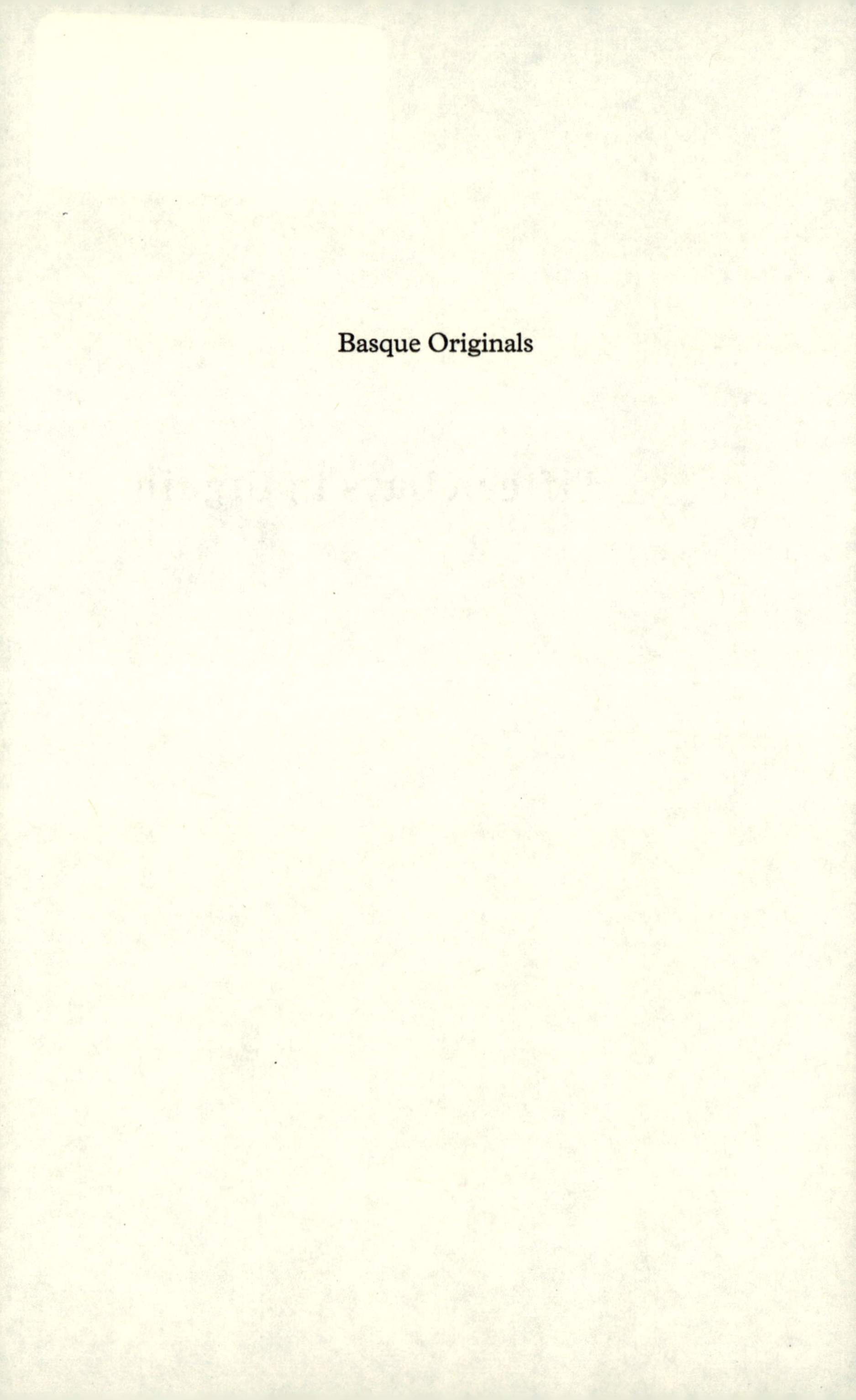

Basque Originals

# 15 Days in Urgain

Jose Antonio Loidi Bizkarrondo

Translated
by Nere Lete

Center for Basque Studies
University of Nevada, Reno

*This book was published with the generous financial support of the Basque government and the American Basque community*

The Center for Basque Studies
University of Nevada, Reno
www.basque.unr.edu

Basque Originals Series, no. 3



Book design: Kimberly Daggett
Cover design: Kimberly Daggett
Cover photograph: Daniel Montero

---

Library of Congress Cataloging-in-Publication Data

Loidi Bizkarrondo, Jose Antonio.
[Urgain bi aste. English]
Fifteen days in Urgain : a Basque mystery / written by Jose Antonio Loidi Bizkarrondo ; translation by Nere Lete.
pages cm. -- (Basque Originals ; No. 3)
Summary: "English translation of the first detective novel written in Basque"-- Provided by publisher.
ISBN 978-1-935709-57-2 (pbk. : alk. paper)
I. Lete, Nere, translator. II. Title.

PH5339.L65U713 2014
899'.921--dc23

2014036576

# Contents

# Main Characters

| | |
|---|---|
| Txomin | Urgain's gravedigger |
| Joxepa (Antoni) | Herriburu's maid |
| Maritxu | Herriburu's wife |
| Larrola | Urgain's new doctor |
| Garaidi (Martin) | Private investigator |
| Muñube (Inaxio) | Nephew of Urgain's deceased doctor |
| Inaxi | Txomin's wife |
| Itziar | Garaidi's wife |
| Elurzabal (Pirmin) | Egurmendi's former servant |
| Bixenta | A maid at the inn |
| Manuela | Joxe Jokin's daughter |
| Joxe Jokin | Innkeeper |
| Egurmendi (Joxe) | A rich gentleman in Urgain |
| Patxi | A policeman and Garaidi's friend |
| Joxe Ramon | Garaidi's assistant |

| | |
|---|---|
| Justino | Garaidi's assistant |
| Herriburu | Garaidi's friend |
| Begoña | Muñube's girlfriend |
| "Mulazen" | Muñube's father |
| Karmentxo | Egurmendi's fiancée |
| Amunda | Karmentxo's father |

1

# Thursday: Txomin on Edge

It was an evening in the dead of winter. The streets of Urgain were empty. And truth be told, not surprisingly. It was pouring rain, whirling wind, cold.

Unlike other days at this hour, gone were the playful outbursts of children. Gone, too, were the shouts of youth meandering up and down the streets with their usual comings and goings.

Rain, rain, nothing but rain.

From time to time, when the train from Donostia arrived, the passengers alighting brought a little spark of life to Main Street, but quickly, after exchanging a few words, they said their goodbyes and rushed home. All that remained were the cold, the rain, and the continuous, rumbling chatter of a few young people loitering under a building's archway.

Pouring rain, whistling wind, cold. In this starless evening, right in the middle of the street, lights hung from posts lined up in a row, swinging and flickering vainly, as if they themselves were the stars.

If ever there were an awful day, this was it. Who would choose to roam the streets on a night like this?

Nevertheless, on this desolate evening, a small, ragged man appeared, clicking steadily down the empty pavement.

Those young people, attracted to the light like moths, gathered by the store-windows under the archway; did they see the man? Apparently not.

His head was covered in old burlap that hung all the way down his back; he wore patched pants, the original color of which no one could guess; big, muddy, traditional *albarkas* on his feet and a hoe in his hands.

With shoulders hunched, he scurried as if afraid of getting wet, yet splashed from puddle to puddle, and passed under dripping gutters. Was he even aware of the rain? His face looked daunted, he trembled. He hoped no one would see him.

No. No one seemed to have noticed him.

Moving briskly, soaked to the skin, he arrived at a half-lit street. Once there, he stopped in front of a house with an enormous door, embellished with ornate nails. After looking up and down the street, he cautiously pulled the iron doorbell-chain. Although it emitted a soft chime, like those shy-sounding bells in convents, it was easily heard in such absolute silence. The soft sound startled our small man, Txomin, the humble gravedigger of Urgain. A dog began barking inside the house. Surely a playful dog, it made a not small ruckus! Txomin drew closer to the door while he kept looking left and right out of the corner of his eyes. No answer. Didn't the people inside hear the bell? He could not stay still. He was in complete distress.

Suddenly, as if in pity of Txomin, the storm began to subside and it stopped raining. Txomin couldn't care less.

As he began to pull the chain for a second time, he heard a door open inside. Someone was coming. At last, a window opened upstairs:

"Who's there?" yelled a young woman.

"Joxepa! It's me, Txomin. Is the master home?"

"No! He's in Bilbao."

She started to close the window, leaving Txomin open-mouthed. Then he yelled:

"Is the lady of the house home?"

"Yes, she is, but can you come back tomorrow at a better time?"

"I must talk to her tonight."

"Wait a minute, then!" grumbled the young woman. She shut the window abruptly. She was so rough, so clumsy!

Poor Txomin was alone once again. He had been in that house so many times before. If the upstairs window didn't close right, if the kitchen faucet or the roof leaked, if they needed a mirror hung, if the power had gone out. . . Txomin was good at everything. He was a humble, hard-working man, a good person; everyone in town loved him. It might have been because he was somewhat naïve. He wasn't one to waste his day counting his fingers, but, indeed, he was a little naîve. He worked as hard as an ant, yet always wore the same pair of old pants. It was hard enough to make ends meet so his wife and children did not go hungry.

It had not been that long since he last fixed the lock of the very door in front of which he now stood. As always, the lady of the house had paid him well for his work. Not only had she paid him ten pesetas, but she had fed him breakfast and given him two fatty *txistorra* links to take home.

But now, his legs quivering, about to faint from fright, he did not think of any of that. Forget the *txistorra* on such a night. Forget the tasty chicken legs. *Txistorra*, what nonsense at a time like this. He couldn't wait to get in the house and spill the beans. Burst! That was precisely what he needed to do.

In the meantime the dog kept barking. Although the saying goes, "Its bark is worse than its bite," one who has had his pants torn might say, "at least the barking dogs give you some warning." But Txomin wasn't thinking of such things. No. He was not afraid of that yappy dog.

He kept waiting; the young woman came at last. She opened the door, took the little, ugly dog in her arms and said:

"Come in, Txomin."

"Good evening." He took off his *txapela*, held it in his hand and dragged his burlap hood. He was finally inside though not as soon as he had hoped. Poor Txomin.

"Wipe your shoes at the door," she ordered him, taking the hoe and burlap sack from him. "You are going to mess up all my cleaning!"

The woman addressing him in such a manner was Joxepa, the Herriburus' dependable maid. Txomin followed her commands, dumbfounded, not knowing what to say.

"Let's go upstairs!""Yes, sure . . ."

"What a cold day today, eh?" said Joxepa noticing Txomin shiver.

"Not that bad, but . . ."

"Come in here!"

She ushered him to a room that he had visited many times before. There were so many beautiful things there. It was obvious that this home belonged to rich people. He was in the sitting room. There was nothing like this in Txomin's house. Why would a man like him, who was always doing something, need a sitting room, anyway?

He had been in that room more than once, admiring the table, the big wooden chest, and the beautiful things on the shelves. But right now he couldn't care less if all those fancy things were made out of gold or clay. Who cared? Poor Txomin stood still, nothing but skin and bones, shivering uncontrollably with a blank look on his face, fidgeting with his folded, wet *txapela*.

2

# Anguish of Many

The lady of the house came at once. She was a sturdy forty-two year old, beautiful woman, a little too sturdy in her own opinion. Though well-off herself, she knew how to be compassionate to the less fortunate. She had often assisted the poor. Txomin came to the right place.

"Good evening, Txomin."

"Good evening."

"You're soaking wet!"

"Yes, a little."

"What brings you here at this hour? Is someone sick at home?"

"No, no. We're all fine."

"An accident? Sit down, please."

Txomin was going through the motions. He stared down at the floor in complete silence; not knowing where to begin, he sat down on the edge of a chair. Herriburu's wife quickly sensed his fright and, wondering what was the matter, she did not take her eyes off him.

"I came hoping to talk to your husband," began Txomin, hesitantly, as if in fear.

"Joxepa must've told you that he is in Bilbao."

"Yes, yes but, I . . ."

"He'll be back in a few days. If you would like to come then . . ." she replied in an effort to put him off.

"No, no! We must do something today!"

"What's wrong?"

"Do you know that Mr. Egurmendi died?" blurted Txomin, leaving his fear and shyness aside.

"Yes, I know. Pour soul."

"So," continued Txomin, now warming up, "he'll be buried tomorrow and . . . I went to the gravesite to get it ready and . . . I saw something horrible."

He stopped to catch his breath. Maritxu, Herriburu's wife, kept Txomin in her sight.

"What?" she asked nervously.

"You know that young Egurmendi's wife died a few years ago, right?" began Txomin in a second round. "So, I saw her body and . . . she has a bullet hole in her forehead!"

There, he said it!

"But that's impossible," replied Maritxu, starting to get frightened herself. "A bullet hole? Are you sure you didn't see something else?"

"No, Ma'am, no. Unfortunately, I have seen people killed by gunshots and I'm sure."

"And what do you think?" she asked him again harshly, "that someone shot her?"

"I didn't say that. I just said what I saw. That's all."

"But . . . what you are saying is impossible!" repeated Maritxu. "You must not have seen well in the dark."

"In the dark? Not at all! It was four in the afternoon. No, no, Ma'am. I saw it clearly through some loose boards."

Now both were silent, Txomin calmer, Maritxu more alarmed. Calmness and happiness, like substance and strength, are they created artificially? Will they survive the test of time? As one got calmer, the other more alarmed; as one experienced some relief the other became burdened.

As the saying goes, "Misery loves company."

"It might have happened after she was buried," continued Maritxu.

"I don't think so."

"Then . . ."

"Then . . ." replied Txomin, echoing her and staring at her intensely.

Both were silent again. Maritxu's head was working hard. How could she wrap her mind around that story? She would not have been as startled had he told her he saw witches and ghosts. They had been long-time friends of the Egurmendis and thought they knew them well. How could that woman have been killed by a gunshot? No one had ever mentioned anything like that. It was preposterous even to imagine such a thing. Egurmendi Sr., who passed away last night, was such a church-going man, and his son, now head of the household, such a decent man. How could this be?

It was true that Maritxu had never met this woman because she died before Maritxu came to Urgain. She kept thinking that in order to be Egurmendi's wife (to each its kind) she must have been a good match. Then, how could a bullet have killed her? And for the Egurmendis to have kept it a secret? How could that be?

"My husband will be here tomorrow or the day after and he'll decide what to do," continued Maritxu, as if in a dream.

"Tomorrow or the day after will be too late. When they bring Egurmendi's body to be buried tomorrow morning, anyone will be able see it, and then what?"

"You're right. Then what? Egurmendi won't like it when this gets exposed. But, what can I do?"

"It's your decision, but in my opinion something must be done tonight."

"Oh, Lord!"

Where did Txomin get today's courage? Who was Txomin, the ragged man in town, to tell Herriburu's wife what to do?

It was about four in the afternoon when he stumbled upon the horrible sight, and now it was already past six. During those two hours he had exhausted his brain. He was worn out. It seemed that he left his shyness aside and that he had attained a new manliness. He could hardly recognize himself.

Maritxu was still overwhelmed by the initial

shock. Paralyzed from head to toe. Txomin had brought frightful news.

"You mean tonight?"

Just then, Joxepa knocked softly on the door and entered the room.

"The new doctor is here. He's asking for you," she said, addressing Maritxu.

"Really? Let him in," replied Maritxu, perplexed.

And, looking at Txomin, she continued:

"He's from my town. Our grandfathers were cousins, I believe," she said, while Joxepa went to fetch him.

"God bless you all this evening!" said the elegant man that appeared at once at the door. He was impeccably dressed. And, just as the rooster stands on one leg, so he stood for a moment by the door.

He was the new doctor who had arrived in Urgain four months earlier; as a doctor, good and knowledgeable; as a man, cheerful but, in the opinion of some, dimwitted and arrogant.

"But . . . what's wrong? Are you alright?" he said when he saw Maritxu's baffled face. He stood next to her.

"Yes. I, yes . . ."

"You look so pale."

"I'm sure I do. This is Txomin, he's the town's gravedigger."

And, that was it. She could no longer keep it to herself, she needed to tell it all, first this, and then that . . . She repeated everything Txomin had told her earlier.

After listening to Maritxu's account and though he only knew the Egurmendis in passing, Dr. Larrola was astounded. This was such an unusual situation. Wasn't that family one of the most prominent in town? Wasn't that family well regarded by all? Did they have any enemies?

"What should we do?" asked Maritxu again.

"Call the police . . ." began Larrola.

"We're going to involve the Egurmendis in such a mess!"

"Then, do you prefer to tell him personally?"

"No, no. Good Lord. We would bring him such anguish."

"Then what? Leave it alone?"

"No . . . no . . ." as if saying, "yes . . . yes . . ."

"Then, there's no other option but to call the police."

"The police?" said Maritxu tapping her forehead with her hand. "Wait, wait a minute. Why didn't I think of it sooner?"

She went straight to the telephone. The two men did not take their eyes off her while she made a phone call.

"Is this Mr. Garaidi's home?" she asked. "Is he in? . . . Oh! Is this you, Martin? This is Maritxu, Herriburu's wife . . . Yes, yes, very well. You too? . . . Yes, he's in Bilbao . . . Well, I need your help; could you come? . . . Yes, yes, tonight . . . No, no, we are well! It's something else . . . I'll tell you later

. . . Will you come? . . . Fine, fine, I appreciate it. See you soon. Goodbye."

"He's a good friend of my husband from Donostia," she explained as she joined them, "a private investigator. He's very smart and he's used to this type of situation. He'll tell us what to do. Yes, he will indeed. He said he's on his way. He'll be here in half an hour."

"Then, I am leaving," said Txomin ready to run away.

"No, no. Stay until he gets here."

"I told you everything I know; now you should decide what to do next. I don't want to get involved in any trouble."

"No one will get you in trouble, Txomin. Don't be like that. Wait until Garaidi arrives, you'll be able to tell him what you saw better than I can. Please, Txomin. Let's go to the kitchen. What do you say about having some *txistorra* while we wait for him? He'll be here in no time."

And after asking him not to mention anything to Joxepa, she took him to the kitchen. He wished he weren't there; at a time like this not even a piece of *txistorra* sounded good.

"While your friend is on his way, I am off to see some patients, but I'll be back soon," said Larrola ready to leave once Maritxu was back in the sitting room.

"Don't tell anything to anyone, please."

"No, no. You can rest assured that I won't."

# 3
# Garaidi's First Inquiries

Now in her bedroom, Maritxu felt overwhelmed; so many thoughts flooded her mind as she knelt imploring for help in front of the image of the Virgin Mary. Could what Txomin said be true? She knew he was a little softheaded, but he was so convinced and definite about what he saw. It was going to be horrible. Oh, Lord. The Egurmendis were such good people and . . . killed by a gunshot! Who would have wanted to kill that woman? No one in town really knew her. Maybe someone in the family? Impossible! She shouldn't even think about it. But, how could they not have seen that hole in her forehead at the time? Could someone have done it after she had been buried? Did someone open the casket? Who could have? Why?

"This is overwhelming," she thought to herself, "at least if my husband were here but, no, it had to happen now. What a predicament!"

While Maritxu was lost in thought, Txomin

was in the kitchen, his wheels turning, without much of an appetite. He was overcome by fear. What if they blamed it on him? What if they locked him up? What a nightmare. Inaxi, yes, Inaxi his wife was the one who convinced him to come to the Herriburus' house. He was in the middle of such a mess. He should've kept it to himself. But then, what if anyone saw it the next day? What then? Poor devil! They would say that he kept it quiet because he was guilty and tried to hide it. They would also say that . . . of course. No, no. It was better to do something about it. What a dead end. Where was that gentleman from Donostia? What would he say? Would he believe him?

After an hour had passed, they heard a knock at the door. Txomin was in the kitchen all curled up, his heart racing; Maritxu peered through the window. And, looking through the corner of the window, she spotted a very small car and realized it was Garaidi's fine, little car.

In the meantime, "Hello, Joxepa," said Garaidi when she opened the door for him. "What's new, Rosy Cheeks?"

Although completely surprised to see Mr. Garaidi at such a late hour, she welcomed him cheerfully. He was no stranger at that home.

"Good evening, sir, nothing much. Come in, please." The one entering the house was a young man, about thirty-five. Well-dressed, strong, wide-faced, cheerful. No matter where he was, he always had a smile on his face, he was always happy, but he knew how to solve the most complicated cases. He was very clever.

Joxepa was delighted to see him. There was no comparison between Mr. Garaidi and Txomin, the simpleton in the kitchen. Mr. Garaidi at least knew how to pay compliments. He called her Rosy Cheeks, such a sweetheart! The lady of the house would be happy to see him, too.

"The lady of the house is upstairs. Let's go up and see her."

The Herriburus lived alone in that beautiful house. Although they had rooms downstairs, too, they spent most of their time upstairs. That's where they had the kitchen, the dining room, and most of the bedrooms. On the top floor, they had an attic.

"Is she alone?" asked the visitor while he stowed his *txapela* on a shelf.

"Yes, sir."

In no time, he was in the same room where Maritxu had spent so much time with Txomin earlier.

"Take a seat. She's on her way."

But he didn't feel like sitting and kneaded his hands continuously as he paced the room.

"Hello, Martin! How's the family?" asked Maritxu as soon as she joined him. "I knew it was you as soon as I recognized your car. Are Itziar and the children doing well?"

"Fine, great! In my house, I am the shabbiest one and look at me!" he answered, laughing and pretending he had a big stomach.

Like all well-trained maids, Joxepa closed the door behind her and left the room. It didn't seem like she had caught on to all the tumult around her. The two of them seemed so cheerful!

"What's happened?" asked Garaidi, as soon as she was gone.

Maritxu, her heart pounding, recounted in a few words everything Txomin had told her. He didn't interrupt her once, but, when Maritxu finished, he frowned, and asked:

"What kind of man is this Txomin?"

"He's a good man. A little naïve but good-hearted. He doesn't know how to lie."

"But he could be mistaken. All this could be nothing but a product of his imagination."

"Yes. That's what I thought at first but, he insists. I have never seen him act so stubbornly. This is very out of character for him. Yes, very much so. He's often in our house fixing things and I know him well; he's a hard worker, and, like parsley in cooking, good for everything."

"Even making things up?"

"No, no Martin! This doesn't sound like a made-up story. I wish it did."

"And the doctor, what kind of a person is he?"

"He's new in town. He's my second cousin. We are not that close, but . . ."

"You shouldn't have told him anything."

"It's too late now. He'll be back soon."

Garaidi stared at the floor, pensive.

"So? What do you think?" asked Maritxu nervously. "What can we do? We should do something tonight."

"Calm down," he replied softly. "We can't start off on a wild chase. We first need to consider cautiously everything we know."

It was already eight in the evening.

Meanwhile, Joxepa was in the kitchen doing her chores, eager to know why Txomin had been talking to the lady of the house for so long and at so late an hour. She tried poking him here and there, but that night Txomin kept quiet and she did not get a word out of him. It shouldn't be too hard for him to pretend to be ignorant.

She asked him so many questions.

"Did you come to see if they'll hire your son?" she asked him nosily, dying to know.

"No."

"You're so full of yourself today!" she burst out furiously. "You became a mute all of a sudden? What do you think, that I will go spreading the news all around? How arrogant can you be? I know how to keep a secret!"

"Is that right?"

"Yes! What do you think?"

"There's two of us, then. I, too, can keep things to myself." And he stayed quiet again. That got to her!

Joxepa finally gave up; realizing that she couldn't get a word out of him, she began babbling: about Egurmendi Sr.'s money dealings, about his son's wedding coming up, about all the people who would attend the funeral, about how beautiful the church ceremony was going to be, about how she was going to have to lie to the lady of the house if she were to get out and see anything, that the whole town would be there . . . She kept going at it nonstop. But all Joxepa's yakking didn't move Txomin. Not a bit. He remained unaffected and, on the surface, even-tempered. What was going on between the lady of the house and the gentleman from Donostia? Inside he was burning with curiosity. His wife, Inaxi, was quick to give him advice. Now he had to face the music. Him. All alone. What were the lady of the house and the gentleman discussing?

Meanwhile . . .

"Where does this Txomin live?" he asked her.

"He's here, in the kitchen . . ."

"Is he? Good. Bring him in, bring him in."

Maritxu called for him and soon he was there by the door, holding his *txapela* in his hands, bowing his head, completely cowed, poor Txomin.

"Good evening," he stopped, tongue-tied.

"Hello, Txomin. It's raining buckets outside, eh?" began Garaidi cheerfully and softly. "Nothing but cold and rain . . ."

"If that were all!" thought Txomin, "I would prefer to suffer ten weeks of uninterrupted storms and cold that would freeze my snot, to all this fuss! No kidding!"

"Sit down, Txomin," said Maritxu tenderly. "This is our old friend, the gentleman I told you about earlier. Don't be afraid, he came to help us."

"Yes, Txomin, Maritxu told me everything. It's sure an amazing story. Yes, amazing, indeed. I am not sure, well . . . How could I tell you? Don't you believe that maybe darkness, perhaps some dirt . . . impeded what you saw?"

"No, sir, no. I am certain."

"And, what did you do?"

"What did I do? Nothing," began Txomin, his eyes wide open and looking at Maritxu as if begging for help. "I didn't do anything! I don't know anything. I only told you what I saw!"

"I don't mean that, Txomin," said Garaidi calmly, sensing what Txomin had imagined. "I mean, what did you do after seeing what you saw in the grave?"

"Nothing, sir. I left everything as it was, told my wife I was headed here, . . . and I came."

"Your wife also knows about it, then? You shouldn't have told her anything. The fewer people that know about it . . . Oh well, now . . ." He stood up. "Let's see what we can do. No one should see us together; you go ahead and wait for me by the gate of the cemetery. I'll follow you. I know the way there."

And poor Txomin did as he was told; he headed toward the cemetery quietly. There was no need to ask him to keep quiet!

"When is that doctor coming?" began Garaidi again, eager to start doing something. "Does he have many friends in town?"

"I don't believe so. He's new in town and . . ."

"Is he a friend of the Egurmendis?"

"No."

They stayed quiet, deep in thought, foreheads wrinkled. Garaidi asked her a few more questions, carefully, but he didn't feel like talking much, he had too many things to think about; they remained quiet for quite a while.

# 4

# Garaidi's Initial Investigations

Out of breath, Larrola arrived at last. He appeared to have come on the run, yet he looked as arrogant as always. Garaidi's first impression of him was not a good one. What a jackass! However, hoping to appeal to his good sense and win him over, Garaidi greeted him cordially. He was afraid that, if left to himself, the doctor might betray Maritxu's confidence. So, after exchanging a few pleasantries, they headed toward the cemetery.

"Don't worry, Maritxu," said Garaidi as he was leaving. "We'll take care of it. Don't worry, and don't let your imagination run away with you!"

'That's right, that's right. Don't let your imagination run away with you," repeated Larrola, full of himself.

Garaidi almost kicked that blowhard, but it was not the time for that.

By then it was past nine and the streets of Urgain were completely deserted. It had stopped raining, but it was bitterly cold. No wonder no one was out.

After they left the village behind and were headed up the road toward the cemetery, they crossed paths with a man on his way down.

"Hello, Muñube," Larrola greeted him as soon as he recognized him. "I can't see your family tonight because I'm in the middle of something." And in short order he introduced Garaidi.

Garaidi wanted to ask him where he was coming from, but decided not to.

"Goodbye, Muñube!"

They continued up the road.

Garaidi didn't say anything, hoping that Larrola would tell him about Muñube, but Larrola kept quiet.

Even before their legs had warmed, they arrived at the cemetery. Txomin was already standing by the gate, still unable to shake his fear. Without uttering a single word, he quickly led them to the Egurmendi family mausoleum. Using Garaidi's flashlight, they looked around the grave and soon were quietly on their way out.

Once they reached the gate, looking for an excuse to stop, Garaidi began cleaning the muddy soles of his shoes with clumps of grass.

"So? What do you think?" he asked Larrola.

"It's a bullet hole. It entered through the forehead and exited through the neck," he answered, conceitedly.

"Or maybe it entered through the neck and exited through the forehead," Garaidi interrupted. "How long ago did it happen?" he asked, pretending the answer was important.

"At least . . . ten . . ."

"Would you like," interjected Txomin, "to come in to my house to warm up a little?"

"Thank you, Txomin, but it's very late. Someone may need Dr. Larrola and I still have to go back to Donostia. Txomin, listen carefully. Right now, right away, take your hammer, some rusty nails, and nail the loose boards of the casket so no one can see inside. I'll be here early tomorrow morning, before anyone shows up. If I'm not here, pretend nothing is wrong; as if nothing had happened, do what you usually do. Most importantly, stay calm."

Txomin's house was a little ways down the road, close to town, and they were already there. Before saying goodbye and leaving, Txomin asked Garaidi:

"Will you come in to calm my wife?"

"Well, a quick in and out."

"I'll wait right here," said Larrola. And he stayed by the door with Txomin.

It was a modest house, though neatly kept.

"Come in, come in!" said Inaxi, Txomin's wife, realizing that the man standing by the door was Garaidi, whom her husband had told her about. "I'm not sure how all this will end up. I wish Txomin hadn't seen anything. What's going to happen to us?"

"Don't worry. Nothing will happen to you."

"Are you sure?"

"Txomin did what he had to do, and what's right is right."

"Yes, but what if someone disagrees?"

"Who, how and why?"

"I am not sure, anyone could . . ."

"No one will. Rest assured and keep tending to your child! What a beautiful baby!" he said, trying to reassure Inaxi and approaching the crib, warm next to the hearth.

"This is Martintxo, our youngest. He's six months old, poor dear."

She gazed at the baby as only a mother can, while she slowly rocked the cradle.

"I'm not sure if I should say this," she hesitated, snapping from her motherly trance, "but, since you're a good friend of the Herriburus, I'll assume you're on our side. You should know everything."

For a moment, as she rocked the cradle, wondering if Garaidi would respond, she remained quiet, but she couldn't let the silence hang any longer.

"This evening," she began again, "after Txomin went to Herriburu's, Pirmin came asking about him."

"Who? Muñube?" asked Garaidi, wanting to

know if she meant the man they saw coming down the road.

"Muñube? No, no, Pirmin, someone who lives in Bilbao. He's originally from Navarre, but he's been Egurmendi's servant for a long time. He came to see if Txomin was home. I told him that he was gone to finish up some chores and that he was going to be home very late. I was trying to come up with excuses so he would leave, but he stayed here waiting for a long time. I was so nervous! At last, completely bored, he left a little before Txomin returned. I didn't tell Txomin anything about it. He left, planning to come back tomorrow. I wouldn't have recognized him if he hadn't told me who he was. I was very young when he left town. Rumor has it that he is a very rich man, now."

"If he were Egurmendi's servant, of course, he must've come on Egurmendi's business, planning to prepare the grave."

"That's what he said."

They warmed to each other. She seemed to be a very sharp woman and surely could keep Txomin in line.

The three men reunited at the doorway and, after reminding Txomin of his duties for the next day, Garaidi and Larrola took off toward town. The trip from Txomin's house was the perfect time to take the doctor down a few pegs. So Garaidi went to work at it, as only he knew how. At last,

Larrola gave him his word that he wouldn't say anything. It was almost eleven by the time he saw the doctor to his door and returned to get his car parked in front of Herriburu's house.

There was light in one of the windows of the house. Maritxu was waiting for him, standing, when Garaidi arrived:

"What was it?" she asked him quietly.

"As Txomin said," he answered as quietly.

"Good Lord!"

"Go to sleep, Maritxu and don't worry."

"Don't worry? God, help us!"

"I'll see you tomorrow."

"I'll be waiting."

He ducked into his car, left Urgain behind and neared Donostia in no time. What a lead foot! Luckily no one else was driving at that late hour, otherwise who knows what could have happened on that narrow road!

"Let's go, let's go home now!" he said to himself, "let's go, let's go!" And he stepped on the gas . . . faster and faster as he kept driving. Why did he need to worry right then? He would have enough time for that after dinner. "Let's go, let's get home!" he repeated to himself.

# 5

# Garaidi Worried

After dinner, as he always did, Mr. Garaidi sat down in a soft armchair in his study and smoked a cigarette while he assessed each of the day's events in turn.

"I have caught many thieves and solved many crimes and mysteries," he thought, "but, Martin, this knot doesn't have a loose end to pull."

To tell the truth, until now he had always had some starting place, some fingerprints left behind, someone without an alibi for the time of the crime, a clue here or there, an accusation, but, whatever it was, he always had a lead to follow. But now . . . what did he have? Nothing much. He didn't even know when that woman had died. He didn't know anything, nothing at all!

The Egurmendis, in Maritxu's words at least, were good people. How could it be possible for one of them to commit such a crime? And still, someone must've laid her in the casket. Was this one person's doing? Were there more people involved? Did Egurmendi see his wife after she died? he wondered. Of course not, he would have been furious! Or, was he the killer?

It could've been an accident, too. Maybe someone fired a gun accidentally while hunting or playing; a stray bullet, perhaps? That must've been it. Why not? That must've been the reason the Egurmendis wanted to keep it a secret. Maritxu was right when she asked him to be discreet. Why would they be the ones spreading the news about that tragedy? But, what if keeping it a secret wasn't the right thing to do? What if she had been murdered? It wasn't going to be easy but, that killer, be it a dog or a cat, wasn't going to escape from him. No way!

After talking to Maritxu, could he be certain that this was a crime committed by the Egurmendis? Of course not! And who could have done this outside of the Egurmendi family? Maybe one of his servants? Maybe . . . Pirmin?

He would not have stood up as quickly as he did, had a mosquito or a snake bitten him. All of a sudden, a thought occurred to him. He was beside himself.

He stepped to his bedroom and told his wife, who was half asleep:

"I am leaving again, Itziar."

"But, where now?"

"To Urgain."

"You just got back from there. When are you going to sleep?"

"It doesn't matter. I'll sleep next week."

Itziar rolled over, covered herself well and lay there, smiling.

There he was again, on his way to Urgain driving even faster than before. Was he going to arrive on time? Before something went wrong? He was so worried. Was Pirmin the killer? He could be, sure. Now that he thought about it, why did he go looking for Txomin? To fix the grave as he thought initially, or to try to cover what Txomin saw? Cover, cover . . . And how could he cover what Txomin saw? How was he planning to keep Txomin quiet? As the saying goes: Only another nail can force a crooked one from the board.

How did he not think of this sooner? He had been so stupid, so stupid! He could never forgive himself if something happened to poor Txomin! How stupid could he be?

He was driving very fast, doing his best not to run head-on into a roadside tree and kill himself. "I am such a stupid fool!" he kept telling himself. And it was true; he should be ashamed of his stupidity. He left Txomin alone in imminent danger. Facing the horns of the bull alone. How could he have done it! And he thought himself a smart man.

He was soon entering Urgain. He thought it would be too obvious if he drove, so, before he arrived at the cemetery, he left the car on the side of the road and continued on foot. He was headed straight to Txomin's house. "If only I could fly!" he kept thinking. He wanted to go faster, to run, but he was afraid of bumping into someone he preferred to avoid, and thinking why he should and why he shouldn't, he continued on, walking as fast as he could.

As he got closer, his heartbeat got stronger. Not because he became tired but because Txomin's imminent danger worried him.

Suddenly, though he was still quite far away, he saw the light on inside Txomin's house. How would they be doing? He knew that, though not visible in such darkness, ahead of him, a little further from Txomin's house, there was the entrance to the cemetery, and, though he didn't know what he would see or do once there, he was headed in that direction.

When he was about forty meters from Txomin's house . . . creeeeaaaak! . . . He heard a squeaking sound and quickly realized it was the iron gate of the cemetery.

He stopped in his tracks, stiffened and, like moss to a rock, remained there standing, glued to the ground. Who was there? Was it Txomin or Pirmin?

Right where he was, by the road, he crawled inside a bush. He was surrounded by darkness and couldn't see anyone but there was someone out there. His hiding place wasn't very comfortable but he could see Txomin's door very well from there; he was silent. What uneasiness! Each minute that passed seemed an hour. In order to have a better vantage point, he moved a little, and a drop of rain trickled down from a small branch to the back of his neck making him shiver from inside out. What a way to shiver!

Just to make sure, it was there, he felt the pistol he always carried with him in his pocket. He preferred not to have to use it but . . .

Now he could clearly hear the footsteps close by. Someone was headed toward him in the dark. Was it Txomin, who didn't need any light because he knew his way around, or was it Pirmin, avoiding being seen? Garaidi wasn't easily scared, but he was very frightened now. He was alert, hunched in the bushes, quietly waiting, yet, ready to come out and reveal himself if necessary.

And, at last, though not as soon as he had wished, the person wandering about neared the house and there, in the light coming from one of the windows, he recognized Txomin. What a relief! Of course, he was back from finishing what he had asked him to do. Reliable Txomin, oblivious to how worried Garaidi had been for his well-being.

Txomin entered the house quickly. And now, what was he doing inside that bush? He came out. Pirmin could still show up at anytime and . . . he had to watch after Txomin. But why was he still hiding by the road? Though it wasn't raining then, the weather was quite unpleasant.

He quickly decided what to do next. In normal circumstances, it would not be the right time to knock on anybody's door, but since he knew he wouldn't be waking anyone, he inched to the house and, toc-toc, knocked on the door. There was some noise inside the house, soon the little light visible through the crack of the window went out and then . . . nothing, complete silence.

His knocking hadn't been a soft one. Surely, Txomin must've had heard it. And yet . . .

Garaidi quickly figured out what was going on. Yes, yes, Txomin must've been scared to death. Of course . . . completely frightened!

"Txomin!" he yelled. "It's me, Garaidi. Open the door!"

A small window up there opened, creaking.

"It's just me, Txomin. Don't be afraid."

"I'm coming, I'm coming!"

As soon as the door opened, Txomin asked frightfully:

"What? Is something wrong?"

"Nothing's wrong, Txomin, nothing at all! I was driving my car," lied Garaidi, ". . . and before I arrived at Amaseta . . . plaf! The car died. I checked this and that, but nothing. I touched this, touched that, but, everything I did was of no use. I had to leave the car behind, not knowing what was wrong with it. And, Txomin, how was I going to start looking for a place to stay in Urgain at this hour? I was planning on returning in a few hours anyway and . . . Pardon me, Txomin, for bothering you but . . . if you would allow me to sleep here, a chair would do . . . Have I disturbed you?"

"No, no! Come in, come in!" said Txomin, believing everything Garaidi said. "I finished what you asked me to do and I just got home."

"Really?" asked Garaidi. "And did it turn out well?"

Garaidi looked so trustworthy. Why wouldn't Txomin have believed him?

"I think so," said Txomin. "Come in, come in! Inaxi will fix your bed in no time."

"Yes, of course," she said as she joined them at the door. "I'll make your bed right now. With all this mess, I won't be able to sleep tonight. I was already in bed awake and I heard everything: Txomin coming in, your knocking, and the rest."

Why did she say "the rest" with a subtle smile? Didn't she believe Garaidi's lies, like Txomin had? That woman was sure sharp!

"Don't worry about anyone suspecting anything," said Txomin when Inaxi left. "Even if a policeman comes with a 'Croscope,' or whatever that instrument is called."

"It will be enough if those who come tomorrow don't notice anything out of the ordinary, Txomin. You just do what you usually do and after that . . . See you later!

"I hope you're right!"

"And . . ."said Garaidi after a while, "has anyone showed up?"

"No. Who was supposed to come?"

"No, no. Just a question."

Inaxi came right then to let him know that the bed was ready. And, since it was late and they had to get up early in the morning, with no more to be said, they wished each other goodnight. Garaidi headed to his room and the other two entered their room, but not without Inaxi thinking of Garaidi's wife. What would she say when she realized her husband never came home?

"Don't worry, she's used to it," he explained.

If she only knew that he had hugged her at home an hour earlier!

As soon as he closed the door, Garaidi turned off the light and walked to the window. He liked the fact that his room was above the doorway of the house. It was the perfect location to keep an eye on everything. The gate of the cemetery, in complete darkness at that hour, was right in front of him and the door of the house, right under his window. What a perfect place to keep watch. The perfect lookout!

After he wrinkled the sheets and messed up the bed so it looked as if he had slept in it, he sat by the window comfortably. Hours came and went, his eyes open sometimes and closed other times, now listening intently and then even more so, in case anyone showed up, always alert; the night went by.

# 6

# Friday: Pirmin, Pirmin!

These were long hours! His way of life often left him in situations like this but he didn't mind. He loved unexpected things. Yes, indeed. His work was very satisfying and exciting.

Nothing happened during the night. Early in the morning, at sunrise, four or five farmers came down the road, most-likely headed to the market in Urgain. Then, nothing. By the time the day broke, a strong, serious, dark-skinned, well-dressed man showed up from the direction of the village. He didn't look menacing but there was something about him. Garaidi perked up and stood. When he got up, after having sat for so long, he felt his buttocks had numbed and, while he rubbed them, he kept watching the man's movements through the window for a while. Who was that man? At that time of the day? Looking like that! In such a place!

In that early morning, in that reddish-light

of dawn, the man soon reached the front of Txomin's house. While continuously looking from the corner of his eye he walked to the gate of the cemetery, which was clearly visible by now. He shook the iron gate back and forth, realizing it was locked. He remained there, looking up and down as if he didn't know what to do next. He then lit a cigarette and began to smoke. His behavior was interesting. Was that Pirmin? He looked like he would be a tough fighter.

Suddenly, hearing someone in the kitchen, Garaidi opened the door and headed that way.

"Good morning, Inaxi!" he greeted her. "Did you sleep well?"

"But, are you already up?" she replied with surprise. "I thought you were still asleep."

"I slept fine, Inaxi. I did indeed, in such a bed!"

"I'm sure you're used to better ones."

While they were chatting, he thought that the man in front of the house might leave and he asked her abruptly:

"Inaxi, do you recognize that man who is scouting the surroundings and standing in front of the house?"

"What? There's someone out there?" she replied fearfully, while the cup she was drying fell from her hands.

More work to do. Another mess to clean up!

"Inaxi, don't be afraid. He's not a thief."

"I'm not scared of thieves. There's nothing of value they could take from my house."

She could not control the urge to run to the window. She was there in an instant compelled by her curiosity.

"It's Pirmin!" she said, her heart rising as soon as she saw him. "The same man who came yesterday. He said he would come back, but I didn't think he would be here at the break of dawn. I wonder what he is looking for at this hour. My good lord! What a predicament! "

She ran to get Txomin and they were both next to Garaidi in a flash.

"Txomin," asked Garaidi, "did you leave the grave like I asked you?"

"Yes, sir. No one would believe that it was fixed yesterday. Don't worry. I worked there for at least two hours."

"Then this is what we need to do next . . ."

He explained everything in a few words. Txomin would head toward the cemetery, pretending he was going to fix something. Most likely Pirmin would approach him to ask about the Egurmendis' grave. Txomin would cheerfully take him there. And if he did his job as well as he said he did the night before, and if Garaidi was right about what Pirmin's plans were . . .

"And if he has other plans? And he does something to Txomin?" interrupted Inaxi, frightened.

"I will be there hiding and I won't allow it.

Don't be scared, everything will be fine. And, most importantly, do not under any circumstances," he told Txomin, "don't let him know that I am here."

"God help us!"

Everything went as Garaidi had predicted. As soon as Txomin emerged from the house with his most innocent-looking expression, Pirmin approached him in an unctuous way.

"Good morning there!" he greeted him. "Are you the gravedigger? I am glad to meet you. Are you the son of Juan Mari who used to be in charge here? We used to talk so often. I take it he died? May he rest in peace!"

Txomin did not have to feed him any lines to continue the conversation.

"Yesterday, I asked your wife about you. I am sure you know who I am. I'm Pirmin, the former servant of the Egurmendi family. I came to make sure his grave looks good for the funeral. Are you headed that way? If you don't mind, we could walk together. The son is so sad. It's not surprising; he is left all alone now."

Eventually, one of them talking nonstop and the other one wishing he were a mute, with Garaidi by the gate, lurking behind a tree or from the shadow of an old wall, they made it to the cemetery and back. Pirmin thanked Txomin, and by his looks, completely at ease, headed toward town at last. Apparently, he didn't suspect anything.

Txomin was so relieved! Inaxi, by the window, had been crossing herself and imploring God all along. Garaidi couldn't have been happier.

"You sure know how to keep your cool," said Inaxi when the three of them came together.

"Why get scared?"

"Oh, what an evil man that Pirmin is!" said Inaxi again. "It seems impossible that such a proper man could be capable of taking away a woman's life!"

"Who told you that?"

"Wasn't he the one who did it? Otherwise, what did he come here for?"

"Wait, wait a minute, Inaxi. We can't say that yet with what we know. Don't be afraid. Don't worry and enjoy your breakfast. I have lots of things to do and I have to go. See you later . . ."

"But, you're not having breakfast with us?" began Inaxi, wanting to show her gratitude.

"No, no. Thank you."

"At least a little bit of milk."

"Thank you, Inaxi. See you soon. Bye."

And with that, he took a side path and went toward town. It was eight in the morning. On the roadside grass blades and bush branches were covered in shiny dewdrops; puddles here and there, too many rocks and too much mud.

Nevertheless, Garaidi was very happy, light on his feet and whistling along, stepping from rock to rock, going toward town, so happy in that early morning. He had a great lead on his hands . . .

It was a beautiful day! A great morning!

Pirmin, Pirmin . . . What else was there?

7

# Joxe Jokin's Endless Conversation

Among all the inns of Urgain, one was the most elegant; Joxe Jokin, a funny, talkative old man, who knew all that went on in town, was the inn's owner. He was a widower who lived with his spinster daughter. What a pair, one an unstoppable chatterbox, the other, as tight-lipped as they come. The father had always been talkative and, naturally, the daughter learned to keep quiet early in childhood. Many wondered what would happen when the father died. All she needed to say to her suitor was "yes" but rumor had it that she stayed unmarried due to her essential silence. No husband, no children, nothing to say, all she did was work at the inn's many chores. She was a diligent, neat, trustworthy woman. All who stayed at the inn were satisfied guests.

It was too early in the morning to go to Herriburu's house, and it was going to be too late to make a round trip to Donostia after mass. So Garaidi decided he would head to the inn once he had a shave and freshened up at the barbershop.

When he arrived at the inn, he came across a maid scrubbing the floor in the entryway.

"God bless!"

"Good morning, sir. *Etxekoandre*!" she yelled, turning toward the interior of the inn.

"Working hard this early, eh?"

"Yes, I am," she replied. "Ma'am!" she yelled again.

Soon she was at the door.

"Good morning, *etxekoandre*. Can I have breakfast?"

"Come in."

Without uttering another word, she led the way and ushered him to a dining room on the first floor.

The room looked lovely. Each table was covered with a white tablecloth and complemented with a vase full of flowers. On one side of the room, a big grandfather clock, which sometime ago, had fallen silent at two o'clock, as had Manuela. On the other side of the room, shelves hung with stacks of china to set the tables. The room had two doors and three windows; everything looked clean and neat.

They quickly brought him a cup of steamy broth and two fried eggs and he began to eat. He had many things to think about.

Leaving Txomin alone last night had been a

stupid decision. How irresponsible of him. Thank God nothing had happened to Txomin, but he felt uneasy about that character Pirmin. Inaxi had said it well. What was he doing at that early hour? What triggered such curiosity? He didn't need to be there at the break of dawn to make sure the grave looked right. He must've had something else in mind. He must've known what information the grave concealed. Yes, that was it. He had to watch Pirmin's comings and goings closely and those of Egurmendi, too. What if both of them were together on this? It could be.

What was he supposed to do? Should he report this Pirmin fellow and have him arrested? Wait, wait a minute, not yet.

And Egurmendi, what was he like? He had come to Urgain many times but had yet to meet him face to face. They spoke highly of him at the barbershop, as did Maritxu. But, without knowing more than he did so far, he could not say anything.

On the other hand, would that doctor keep quiet? He promised he would and Garaidi needed to believe it.

After he finished his breakfast, he crossed his legs and, while half-asleep, mulling over what he had learned, an old man shuffled up to him.

"God bless and enjoy your food."

Garaidi recognized him right away because he had seen him before, during the town festivals.

Toothless, with an elongated nose and chin, white hair and wrinkled skin, those lively eyes, his rather hunched-back . . . It was Joxe Jokin, the innkeeper. Oh no, he was doomed! This was the most talkative man alive!

"Unlike yesterday, it looks like we're going to have a beautiful day today. Wasn't yesterday's weather dreadful?" he said mumbling. He rested his cane on a chair, and after taking a couple of plates from the shelf, he sat at another table. It looked like he was ready to have breakfast himself.

"Yes . . ." answered Garaidi, a bit dryly.

"At least it stopped raining!"

Garaidi was quiet. He had better things to do than waste his time talking to the old man.

"You must've come to Urgain for Egurmendi's funeral."

"Yes, sir."

"You sure came early enough."

"Yes. I didn't know when the services were for sure," lied Garaidi.

"You're not from around here, are you?" said Joxe Jokin, fishing for a conversation topic. Did he ever fail to find one?

"No, sir, from Donostia."

"Donostia, Donostia, ai, ai, ai . . . just like here, the leaves only sprout once a year there, too," he said in an effort to demystify Donostia. "Beautiful place Donostia, I agree, very beautiful, sure, but a little too big. That's too bad. Urgain is not envious of Donostia at all! Donostia people would prefer Urgain's peace if they were given the choice. My friend, I can't understand how you all can put up with such chaos and deafening noise. Yes, I must admit that you have a beautiful beach but, if you ask me, I would prefer a glass of hard cider under the shade of an ash tree in the Ameseta grove to roasting under the sun."

Now he had found a conversation topic.

"Did I mention it's a little too big?" He kept on non-stop, sounding like a horn. "Let me clarify what I mean."

He was holding his cane between his legs as he placed his hands on its knob and his chin on his hands, calmly, like *Olentzero*, and kept talking on and on:

"God has made us to live in harmony with each other in this world. If we hold on to this togetherness, we will get to know each other better and we'll achieve complete brotherhood and friendship. But, listen to me carefully, my friend; how will we become friends living in the same town if it's so huge that we don't even have a chance to meet? You tell me. I have lived in America, in Buenos Aires. What a beautiful city. It sure was. Oh my! It was at least a thousand times the size of Urgain. There were so many different types of people, and yet, I . . . I was lonelier than I'd ever been in Urgain. Why? You want to know why? Because amid all those people, I didn't know anyone well enough. Yes, you see? And do you know what was the worst? Anywhere I went, yesterday and today, tomorrow and the next day, here and there, at home and on the streets, day after day, I needed to prove I was a decent man. Goodness Gracious! Who could last there? I couldn't wait to return to my birthplace. The worst thing wasn't to be repaid with an insult for a favor or to do a good deed and be slapped in return, no, the worst was to need someone's help, to go to them and have to prove you were worthy of their assistance. You had to explain where you were coming from, where you were headed, who knew you, what you did for a living, where you lived . . . What a headache! And, on top of everything, you needed to be grateful if they believed you. Let me tell you . . . In Urgain, on the other hand, most of us know each other. If someone approaches you in need, you know what that person is like. If you need something yourself, you know where to go. That is priceless peace of mind, don't you agree? Let me tell you, it is. It is work to be a decent person, but here, that is our only job. Back there it wasn't enough to be good; you had to prove your decency to everyone constantly. And, when you remained quiet because you had gotten tired of it, they would immediately cast you aside as if you were a liar, one more of so many others."

They brought him breakfast, too, and he began to eat. But that did not slow him down. Would he finally shut up for a triviality such as eating breakfast? Not a chance, no way.

"Speaking of which," he kept at it with his mouth full, "this reminds me of what a man in Argentina told me once. This is what that thick-skinned guy told me:

'Do you want to tell the decent people from the crooked? It's easy. Curse without mercy at all who come to you asking for money and send them away. Those that return will be the mean, the lazy, and the freeloaders; those who do not return will be the good, the decent, and the humble.' But then, I told him, 'if the ones who are truly in need don't come back, how can you help them?' He couldn't care less! So . . . you are from Donostia, eh? Ai, ai, ai . . . Listen now. Last week, 'Big Pellu' passed away here, in Urgain. Do you think anyone will miss him? Not a bit. He was nothing but a lazy bum, a gambler and a drunk. Egurmendi's death yesterday, on the contrary, will sadden the entire village. Such was his stature. And, while he lived among us, unlike me in America, he didn't need to show us constantly his decency badge. By the same token, no one would be surprised, after loaning five bucks to Big Pellu, if the debt were left unpaid. No one would have lent him any money to start with. Of course not! We all knew what they were like. No one would've mistaken Egurmendi for 'Big Pellu.'"

Joxe Jokin was rolling now, blah, blah, blah,

enjoying himself.

On and on, he could even put a trout to sleep. After spending all night awake, Garaidi himself was half asleep, but perked up as soon as he heard Egurmendi's name mentioned. Joxe Jokin complimented Egurmendi profusely, but never mentioned anything about that woman at all. Was Egurmendi the great man that everyone thought?

"In America," he prattled, "don't think I don't know how things are, my friend. They do everything backwards. You see . . . it's burning hot at Christmas time and, in July, nothing but ice and snow. Can you believe it? That says it all."

That said it all? If only that were true. He kept at it, non-stop, for what seemed like forever. He kept talking even with his mouth full. He was incessant. What a filibuster! Would he ever stop? Who knew?

Fortunately, an acquaintance came in; otherwise . . . Garaidi had met this man the night before on his way to the cemetery with Larrola. It was Mr. Muñube.

"Hello! Good morning! We meet again today?" he greeted while shaking Garaidi's hand. "Did you stay here overnight?"

"No, I just came," he answered, happy since Joxe Jokin had finally stopped his rambling. "The man of the house was just telling me some stories."

"I bet he was! Most likely half of them were lies and . . ." began Muñube when Joxe Jokin cut him off:

"Half of them lies, eh?"

After he swallowed a fist-size piece of bread dipped in milk, bobbing his head up and down like chickens do, he resumed, this time half-singing:

"In place of the truth,
men's lies repeat.
Dogs chew on bones,
and leave the meat.
It's not a very even match
To trade a human for a beast."

And without taking a break, he continued:

"I tell lies? I'm always the liar, the blabbermouth. You pin it all on me! What about you? You, who's nothing but a bum! This reminds me of something that a workman I had in America once told me."

"Which you have told a hundred times already. That's old news!"

"I've told you a hundred times? That's a lie. I may have started telling the story a hundred times but . . . have I ever finished it? I don't believe so! Now you'll need to listen to it even if you'd rather not. In America . . ." he resumed as he moistened his lips with his tongue and stared at Garaidi, ". . . one hot day, at noon, we had to move some home furniture on a truck and the workers were taking their time bringing the loads up to the bed of the truck. Gentlemen! What laziness! Three men began lifting a big, heavy box . . . 'ugh!' They couldn't. 'Ugh . . . !' Nothing again. 'Let's go, guys! Ughhhh!' They couldn't do it. I got tired of looking at those loafers, so I pushed them aside, took the box and, boom! I lifted it to the truck by myself. That was some power! I stood in front of them, my legs in a wide stand resting my hands on my thighs, gazing at them sharply as if telling them, 'have you seen how it's done, lazy bums?' And do you know how one of them responded? 'Sure, anyone could do it that way!'"

The two-man audience burst into laughter. But, before they had even closed their mouths, Joxe Jokin started chatting away again. His stories were remarkable, but . . . were they really listening? Garaidi had plenty to think about. Muñube, as was obvious by his palpable uneasiness, must've had something on his mind, too.

Finally, Joxe Jokin stood.

"Oh, my!" he said unable to straighten. "My right knee is acting up."

"That's old age, Joxe Jokin, old age!" said Muñube.

"What old age are you talking about? Are you showing off today, eh? My left leg is just as old as the right one and it's not mocking me!"

There was nothing worse than mentioning old age in front of Joxe Jokin. He, old? Preposterous! He was only about to turn eighty-two.

"Now that you are no longer alone," said Joxe

Jokin, looking at Garaidi, "I'm going to feed the chickens."

"It would be better if you brought us one for lunch," said Muñube smiling.

"One chicken for ten of us?" Joxe Jokin said. "One chicken, he says!"

And once again, half-singing like before:

"I have one rooster
in a ten chicken coop.
One rooster won't satisfy
ten hungry mouths.
I'm telling you."

At last, the old man left the same way he had come, shuffling his feet and rubbing his lips with the back of his hand. Still, when he reached the door, he turned to Garaidi and Muñube and added:

"Oh my! I pity the fate of those that must go down the throat of others!"

"Finally, peace!" thought Garaidi when the chatterbox left. But his counterpart did not look very much at peace. As soon as Joxe Jokin closed the door, Muñube walked right up to Garaidi's table.

"I wanted to talk with you . . ." he began.

# 8

# Muñube Blurts It Out

"With me?" replied Garaidi, surprised. "What's the matter?"

It was not easy to guess how old Muñube was. At times, one could think that he looked like a prematurely-aged young man, one who had endured a harsh and messy life. Other times, he looked like a health-conscious fifty-year-old. But he was truly forty. His hair was graying, salt and pepper, and his eyes were lined with wrinkles. He was a clean-cut, good-looking man. In the opinion of some, he seemed too preoccupied with his looks; for others, too self-centered.

"I'm not sure how to begin,"he said. "I'm Larrola's friend."

"Sure, he introduced us last night."

"Right. Larrola came to Urgain through my family to replace my uncle. That is how we know each other. My uncle and Mr. Egurmendi, who passed away yesterday, were friends since childhood. They visited each other frequently. I'm not sure if you knew him."

It was obvious that he was having a hard time getting to the point. But finally he said:

"About eighteen or twenty years ago, a young man named Pagodi lived in town. Have you heard of him?"

Garaidi shook his head and Muñube continued:

"No one found out what happened to him, but he suddenly disappeared without leaving a trace; no one knew where he went, or even if was alive or dead. No trace of him what so ever. His parents have since passed, as have all his relatives."

Garaidi didn't know anything about this and he listened attentively.

"Do you know," he continued, "what my uncle, once he lost his mind, repeated while on his deathbed? 'Pagodi's disappearance is Egurmendi's fault, it's Egurmendi's doing.' "

"How?" Garaidi asked, wanting to know more since, once again, Egurmendi's name came up.

"I have often heard of you," Muñube said, changing the subject. "I know that you are very good at solving mysteries and I've thought of contacting you more than once but, not knowing you personally, I hesitated. Having you here, though, makes things so much easier. Those Egurmendis!"

"Then, you think they are involved somehow?"

"Something like that."

"You think they killed him?"

"That, or they made him disappear for some reason."

"And, who assassinated him?"

"I told you what my uncle said."

"But you said it yourself, he'd lost his mind by then."

"You're right, but you know that sometimes people on their deathbeds confess the biggest truths."

"Even if you were right, there's nothing I can go on," said Garaidi, not sure of what Muñube was looking for. "What do you want me to do after all these years?"

"Find Pagodi," he answered with conviction.

"What's in it for you?"

"To find out if what my uncle told me was true."

"Does this mean you want to hire me?"

"Yes."

"Are you going to pay me for my work, then?"

"Yes."

"All right, Muñube, all right," said Garaidi getting off his chair. "I'm on my way to Egurmendi's funeral now, but come by my house anytime and we'll talk calmly about this. I'll do what I can . . . Do you live here?"

"Yes, right here, at the inn."

"Good. See you soon."

What was this new mess in which the Egurmendi family seemed to be involved, now? Was this a case where appearances were deceiving?

"These latest accusations and the graveyard situation," Garaidi thought,

"Why was Muñube interested in finding Pagodi? If this were so important for him, why didn't he do something about it sooner? His sudden urgency seemed strange. Was he plotting something when we saw him on his way back from the cemetery? Or did Larrola tell him something? Was that it?"

While lost in thought, Garaidi arrived at Maritxu's house. She was headed to church, too, and, once she finished getting ready, they left together.

"I have lots of information to share with you, Maritxu, and some questions to ask you, too," said Garaidi on their way to church. "But I shouldn't say anything now. I need something more. What a night I've had!"

Among all the out-of-town attendees, no one at the church or at the graveside service seemed to notice Garaidi. The villagers thought he was a relative of the Egurmendis'; some relatives thought he was some cousin's friend, others, a friend's cousin. Same difference.

Nothing out of the ordinary happened in church or at the cemetery. Txomin acted as if he didn't know anything, though he hid his fear inside. Inaxi stayed home, observing everyone carefully from behind her window. Garaidi recognized Pirmin who didn't leave Egurmendi's side. Egurmendi seemed to be a nice man. He looked pale, sad and sorrowful, shaking hands with people. Garaidi stayed out of his way so he could watch him better later without being recognized.

Larrola did not attend any of the services. He must've gone to see a patient or, maybe, he was overcome by fear.

By noon they were back at Maritxu's house.

There was a burning smell coming from the kitchen. It was the result of Joxepa's curiosity . . .

# 9

# Good Thing She Died!

Even though the bean soup would be burned, Garaidi wanted to ask Maritxu so many questions that he decided to stay for lunch. On one hand, he needed Maritxu's help and, on the other, he assumed Joxepa must've had something else on the stove besides the burned beans.

As soon as they began eating, Garaidi explained what had happened the previous night. He did not mention Pirmin's suspicious behavior, nor did he bad-mouth or say anything against the Egurmendis. He told her half-truths, avoided certain facts and softened others. And, just like that, as only he knew how, he got all the information he needed from Maritxu.

He learned all kinds of information about many people. The Egurmendis were one of the richest families in town; although most of the time they lived in Urgain, they owned houses and land in Donostia, Madrid, and France. They loved Urgain and they worked hard to improve it. After Egurmendi senior's death two nights ago, his son, Joxe, inherited everything, including the beautiful mansion where they lived. Mrs. Egurmendi had died a few years before. They were rich, healthy, and well-regarded by everyone; they did not need anything. This was not a family that rested on their laurels, though they were generous and had dried plenty of tears and lifted many hearts by helping those in need. How could there be a killer among them?

Maritxu said that Joxe Egurmendi, a widower, was planning to marry a beautiful young woman from Urgain. He was forty-two and his fiancée, Karmentxo, twenty-eight; he was rich and she had nothing, but they loved each other. She worked as a seamstress in Donostia and, apparently, though engaged to Egurmendi, she did not quit her job; she did not let Egurmendi's riches go to her head. Everyone agreed that she was a good, humble, and sensible young woman.

She was Muñube's cousin. Although their mothers were sisters, Karmentxo and Muñube were very different. He spent years in Madrid studying medicine at the expense of his uncle, Urgain's former doctor. What for? Nothing. When his uncle passed away, he had to quit his studies and return like he had left for Madrid, empty-handed. His parents who lived in Donostia with one of their daughters refused to pay for his adventures in Madrid. They could not afford it. After his uncle died, Muñube drifted for a few months without employment, but now he worked at an infirmary and lived in Joxe Jokin's inn.

Apparently, a while ago, he had hoped to marry Karmentxo, but she was not interested and rejected him again and again. Muñube had to give up finally. Now he had a young girlfriend in Donostia. Maritxu had never seen them together, but . . .

"And what do you know about someone named Pagodi?" Garaidi suddenly asked. "I've heard that . . ."

"Pagodi? My lord! Those are old stories. I didn't live here in those days, but I heard the gossip from my mother in law. Yes, it was a well-known story."

From what Maritxu knew Pagodi and Egurmendi had been long-time friends. They had been childhood playmates and later classmates. They were together when the outbreak of World War II stranded them in Lovaina. After a great deal of hardship, both finally made it to Urgain.

Maritxu continued with her story, "After days without knowing their whereabouts, they arrived in town. Their families were so relieved. Pagodi left his parents' house saying he was headed to Egurmendi's and that was the last they heard of him. His parents were devastated."

She more or less confirmed what Muñube had told him. But she did not mention anything about the deathbed nightmares of Muñube's uncle. She must not have known anything and, if she did, she did not tell him.

'The Egurmendis said," continued Maritxu, "that Pagodi never made it to their house, and that was it, they left it at that. Rumors ran wild and finally they heard that he had drowned in a river, but nothing was known for sure. It had been difficult for the Egurmendis because that same day, the woman that Txomin recently discovered . . ."

"Died? Egurmendi's wife?" Garaidi helped her.

"They got married in Belgium and he had brought her to town just a few days before her death. They were newlyweds. And . . . now this. Dear Lord!"

"What did they say she died from?" asked Garaidi.

"From Typhus or some other contagious illness, I believe. No one got to see her; they buried her immediately, following the doctor's orders."

Garaidi was all ears.

"Who was the doctor then?"

"Dr. Muñube, who died last July."

"I see."

Was the knot unraveling?

"I thought of something, Martin," began Maritxu, worried. "If that woman had typhus, could she have been walking about in her garden the day before she died?"

"No. The high fever lasts days."

"My mother-in-law told me more than once that she had seen her in the garden the day before she died; she never understood how she could be dead the next day. Every time she talked about it, I would remark, 'poor woman', and we dropped the subject, but she always remained doubtful. She did not understand how that could be. She worried."

"Nonsense," said Garaidi suspecting where she was headed.

"Now I'm worried, too," thought Maritxu.

"I guess Muñube had been well- regarded by all. Apparently, the Egurmendis held him in high esteem, too."

What kind of an illness was this that someone could be fine one day and dead and buried the next? And old Dr. Muñube was in the middle of all of it; surely he knew something.

"Good thing she died," Maritxu said, nodding, her eyes wide open.

Garaidi tried to calm her down by doing his best to ease the trembling that had permeated to her core, but his effort was in vain. All the while he kept thinking about Joxe Jokin's stories, Txomin's panic, Inaxi's observations, Egurmendi's good reputation, Pagodi's dark story, Larrola's arrogant behavior.

"Good thing she died," Maritxu kept repeating.

Lost in conversation, time flew by. Nevertheless, Garaidi kept his suspicions about Pirmin's coming and goings and Muñube's information to himself. No sense sharing them.

"If only I knew what old Dr. Muñube knew!" Garaidi kept thinking. He was afraid that Maritxu was right to say, 'good thing she died.'

10

# Saturday: When They Least Expected. . .

Garaidi was in need of a good night's sleep after having none the previous night. Before he awoke fully and while half dreaming and snoring, his wife, Itziar, came to him.

"Get up, you have a call from Urgain."

He went to the phone quickly.

"Hello?"

It was Joxe Jokin. Was this going to be another one-way conversation? Not again, thought Garaidi.

"What's the matter, Joxe Jokin?"

There had been a burglary at the inn.

"Have they stolen a lot?"

"A lapel pin," said Joxe Jokin.

"Of great value?"

"Not really."

"And what do you want me to do?"

Of course, that old buzzard found out his line of work. Who could've told him? Nothing escaped that old man!

"O.K. Joxe Jokin, O.K. I'm busy now but I'll be there as soon as I can."

What did Joxe Jokin think, that Garaidi could waste his time with such trivial things? Didn't he talk enough yesterday?

"Was the lapel pin yours?"

"Hm. Apparently It was Muñube's."

"Any idea who might have taken it?"

What a question! They suspected Pirmin. Were they right? That was quite an acusation! Now Pirmin was stealing . . . from Muñube. What would be next?

"I'm on my way."

An hour later, Garaidi was in a small bedroom at the Inn. Joxe Jokin gave him all kinds of details about when, how, and where everything happened. He repeated everything forward and back. He was a master at that.

"Last evening, after dinner," he began, ecstatic that he had a great new topic of conversation, and he savored the words as he pronounced them, "we were chatting in the downstairs dining room. And, suddenly, we heard all this bing-bang, pim-pum, tumult on the second floor. What a ruckus! I am quite slow, my feet, you know, but those who were with me rushed upstairs, and do you know what they found? Muñube and another man fighting. The man, named Pirmin, who lived now in Bilbao, was from Nafarroa and had been

Egurmendi's servant. Pirmin was in Urgain for Egurmendi's funeral and was staying at my place for a few days. I've known him for a long time but I didn't realize he was such a good fighter. You need to be good to face Muñube. I once saw a fight when I was in America, and . . .

"How did the fight begin?" Garaidi asked so the old man would not go off the subject.

"Why?" he said, tilting his head, open-mouthed. He only could hear from one ear. "Well . . . I'm not sure, but Muñube said that when he entered his bedroom, he felt someone's presence in the dark. Thinking it was a thief he tried to catch him and broke into fighting. He began throwing blind punches here and there in the dark, at times hitting the target and at times missing it, while the thief did the same. They didn't recognize each other and kept at it for quite a while, throwing punches and hurting each other. It was a big mess. Bruised eyes, wiggling teeth, and a vase on the floor shattered into thousand pieces. I was heart-broken to see the vase shattered like that. My uncle Paustino had given it to me as a wedding gift."

"And?" interjected Garaidi, always keeping on track.

"Simple. Pirmin went into the wrong room, thinking he was entering his own and, at the same time, Muñube thought he was fighting a thief. They both apologized and cleared the mishap, and that was it. They beat each other up for nothing. This reminds me of an old story. When I was in America . . ."

"Joxe Jokin," interrupted Garaidi reaching up with his arms. "What about the burglary?"

"Wait a minute, wait. I haven't been in America for nothing. That Muñube is such a fool. Wait a minute, I also followed the others upstairs," he began, making sure he didn't leave anything out. "When all the ruckus quieted down, I began picking up the broken vase pieces and do you know what I saw right there, laying on the floor?"

"Please tell me," Garaidi encouraged him.

"Muñube's one-of-a-kind lapel pin," answered Joxe Jokin, quietly placing his hands before his mouth like a bugle as he got closer to Garaidi. "What do you think?"

He held his horn to his ear. He displayed a crooked grin, showing his three remaining teeth and, looking sideways, winking, took on the appearance of a witch.

Garaidi remained quiet for a while. What was he thinking about?

"Muñube must've dropped it," he began.

"Muñube? No sir, no! That's the thing. Muñube never wore the pin. He wasn't wearing it, when he went upstairs after dinner, either. And don't tell me he was, because he wasn't. This bad leg slows me down, like a wagon missing a wheel, but..." He was waving his arms like a windmill.

"What did Muñube say?"

"Muñube?" he repeated tilting his head again. "Poor guy, he didn't say anything. He could hardly see anything from that swollen eye. He was busy enough trying to stop his nose bleed. But Pirmin . . . You should've seen how he looked at me when I placed the lapel pin back in its box.

"And, did he tell you anything?"

"No. He asked my daughter for the bill, paid it, and left at once. He didn't even stay for dinner. I can't believe he wanted to steal that pin. "

"And how did Pirmin know about the lapel pin?"

"Muñube showed it to everyone after lunch."

"Did you tell him anything?"

"To that knucklehead? No, I didn't tell him anything. Aren't you glad I didn't?" he asked with a grin, as if he were showing a pretty toy to a child, tilting his head and directing a complicit look at him.

"Joxe Jokin, you should be an investigator."

"You bet. I sure would love to. I feel like I did twenty years ago, my feet faster than a flea."

"Will Muñube show me that lapel pin?" interrupted Garaidi, bursting Joxe Jokin's nostalgia.

What was prompting the urge to see the pin?

"Shut up and come with me."

And Joxe Jokin lead the way upstairs, shuffling his feet; Garaidi followed him in silence. They entered Muñube's room on their tiptoes and Joxe

Jokin took a lapel pin out of a small box. Garaidi's heart flipped. Did Joxe Jokin notice? It didn't seem so.

Truly, astounding, it was Pagodi's pin.

How did Garaidi know about this pin? The day before, after he had lunch with Maritxu, he went to Donostia and spent some time at the library reading newspapers from the time of Pagodi's disappearance. The newspapers, as they did in those days, explained the news from top to bottom with all kinds of detail.

He read about Pagodi's entire life. His father had been a seaman; he had sailed around the world and, on one of those long voyages, he had visited Madagascar; the pin had been made there and, on the occasion of his son's trip to Belgium, his father gave it to him; Pagodi was wearing it when he disappeared; this and that . . . Everything was narrated right there.

Could this pin in front of him be a different one? Impossible. How could there be two identical pins? This pin matched the description given in the newspaper. It had two initials engraved in the inside: 'T. P' Tomax Pagodi, of course. There could not be two identical pins.

"Have you told anyone about this?"

"No, I haven't. And believe me it wasn't an easy task."

"I'm sure, Joxe Jokin, I'm sure. Don't cave in now. Why should we spread the news about this burglary? We should keep it a secret."

Garaidi did his very best to convince Joxe Jokin not to say anything. But would he stay quiet?

"You wouldn't want to lose your inn, would you? You wouldn't want to give your business a bad reputation, I'm sure. Then the best thing you can do is keep quiet. If not, you're doomed."

Yes, he would stay quiet.

The case was a huge mess. On one hand, there was what Txomin showed him at the graveyard. On the other hand, Pirmin's goings and comings. Then, what Muñube told him, and now, what Joxe Jokin unexpectedly shared with him: that Muñube had the pin, which apparently belonged to the long-vanished Pagodi. If that weren't enough, it seemed that Pirmin was trying to steal the pin from Muñube.

It wouldn't be wrong to conclude that all these events were connected, but what was the common thread among them?

Why did they bury that woman in such a hurry? Was it perhaps because they wanted to hide the bullet hole in her forehead? Why did Pirmin go to the cemetery at such an early hour in the morning? What was he trying to hide? It was obvious that he knew something.

Was it true what Muñube told him? Or were these accusations motivated by Karmentxo's rejection of Muñube and engagement to Egurmendi? This seemed a flimsy reason to accuse Egurmendi and to reveal the doctor's deathbed nightmares. Or was there, perhaps, an ulterior motive? He was in possession of Pagodi's lapel pin. Was he trying to blame others for his doings? Muñube knew more than he said. If his uncle were alive, he would be able to clarify everything. Why was Maritxu afraid of him?

But why did that fool, knowing that the pin belonged to Pagodi, carelessly show it to everyone? That had been the wrong thing to do. How imprudent of him. What an idiot! Pirmin had been quick to recognize the pin.

Pagodi disappeared while on his way to Egurmendi's house; a woman killed by a gunshot that same day . . . Yes, everything was connected. But where could he start?

So far, there were three men to keep a close eye on: Egurmendi Jr., Pirmin and Muñube. Whom should he confront first? How could he keep investigating without raising any suspicion?

In any event, he needed to shed some light on the woman's death. First, discreetly as Maritxu had advised, then he would announce the news like the midday church bells. Finally, the answer would thunder like the bells on Urgain's biggest feast day. Garaidi was a determined man. Yes, he was! Where should he begin, though?

When he arrived home at lunchtime, he found a telegram waiting for him:

"Honest, rich. I'll write more later. *Agur.* Patxi."

11

# Slippery Slope

After thinking long and hard about how to proceed with his investigation, Garaidi finally decided to face Muñube that very same afternoon. Truth be told, it was a slippery slope, but, due to the urgency of the situation, he decided to begin with Muñube. That was the right move since Muñube had been the one who mentioned Pagodi's name.

He arrived at Joxe Jokin's inn determined to talk with Muñube. At that time of the evening, it was about nine; men packed the downstairs bar. He joined the rest of the customers while keeping an eye on the door, drinking and listening to the lively conversations of those around him. Thankfully, Joxe Jokin was nowhere to be seen, but his daughter was. She was working diligently. She acknowledged him with a timid 'Hm'. She didn't seem to care about the fistfight that took place the previous night.

Garaidi didn't have to wait long.

"Good evening," he greeted Muñube as soon as he came into the bar.

"Hello."

"I am here to talk to you about what you told me."

"Sure. Would you like a drink?"

"Thank you. Let's go to your room, if you don't mind."

"Yes. Let's go upstairs."

"Any news?" Muñube asked as soon as they entered the room.

"Well . . ." Garaidi began after taking a chair. "You asked me to find Pagodi and, although I haven't found him yet, I found something that belongs to him and that was in his possession when he disappeared."

"Really? What is it?" asked Muñube, wide-eyed.

"A pin."

"A pin? What kind of pin?"

Garaidi, hoping to notice some change in his facial expression, didn't take his eyes off him. He waited in silence, to no avail. Apparently, Muñube wasn't affected by what he heard.

"A lapel pin," he began again, and stopped.

"Where did you find it?"

"Where? Right here," he said looking at the box on the shelf.

"Here? Where?" said Muñube surprised, looking back and forth at the box and Garaidi.

"In that little box."

"But, what are you talking about? How do you know what's inside that box?"

"There's a lapel pin."

"How can this be? Who gave you permission to look inside the box, you snoop?" Muñube erupted, enraged. "That pin is mine!"

"It had been Pagodi's."

"No!"

"Yes!"

"What are you talking about? You're crazy!"

"Here!" said Garaidi, taking a few newspaper clippings out of his pocket that mentioned Pagodi and handing them to him. "Read the news, read as much as you want. You'll see."

He began reading the articles intently. The more he read, the more he worried. He took the lapel pin out of the box and placed it next to the newspaper while he kept looking back and forth at the pin in his hand and the picture in the article. He blushed; he turned pale, then blue; his jaw dropped; his eyes bugged out of their sockets; his fingers trembled . . .

He was plainly aghast. As he kept reading, his mood became more obvious.

"How did you get this lapel pin?" asked Garaidi, when Muñube finished reading the papers.

"This one?" he said staring at the pin he held in his hand. "My uncle gave it to me."

"And why do you look so alarmed?"

"Me, alarmed? Not really. I didn't know it belonged to Pagodi and I'm surprised. That's all. I'm just surprised. Do you think that if I had known it belonged to Pagodi, I would have shown it to everyone yesterday, after lunch?"

"I am aware of that."

"So, how can you think that I stole it?"

"I haven't said that."

"But you implied it."

"You didn't tell me everything you know about Pagodi, did you?"

"I told you everything."

"No, you didn't. You didn't tell me how much you despise Egurmendi."

"I despise Egurmendi? C'mon now! Why would I despise him?"

"Because he's about to marry Karmentxo, whom you loved."

"That and what we are talking about now are two different things."

"In my opinion, they are connected. Besides, you haven't told me how you got that black eye."

"Now you're saying this is connected, too? I got in a fight last night. So what?"

"Did you know the person you fought?"

"I'd never seen him until the day before yesterday."

"He was Egurmendi's former servant," Garaidi said, provokingly, while staring at him.

"Egurmen . . ." began Muñube. He was astounded, dumbstruck.

"Didn't your uncle insist that Egurmendi was involved in Pagodi's story? What if this man from Bilbao is involved, too?"

"Then . . ."

"Yes, Muñube, yes! He was looking for this lapel pin. I'm convinced."

"Rotten thief!" said Muñube, now furious. "They're responsible for Pagodi's disappearance. If I'd known it earlier, if I'd known last night that he'd been Egurmendi's servant, I would've beaten the hell out of him. That ass! If I'd known it!"

"And now," Garaidi began softly, after Muñube let all his anger out, "tell me the truth, where did your uncle get this lapel pin?"

"My uncle?" he said, calming down. "Pagodi must've sold it or given it to him."

Now he looked calm.

"The newspapers mention that Pagodi was wearing it when he disappeared. Haven't you read it? So when do you think he gave it to your uncle?"

"How should I know?" lashed Muñube.

"We must find out. Isn't it remarkable that, after having bad-mouthed Egurmendi, your uncle would end up with the lapel pin?

Muñube was speechless. He couldn't . . . he couldn't tell the truth. Not in a million years!

Garaidi realized that Muñube wasn't saying another word.

"May I borrow the pin?" Garaidi asked, ready

to grab it and leave the room.

But Muñube couldn't bring himself to answer yes or no. He was sitting on the edge of the bed, digging his elbows into his knees, holding his head between his hands, completely dissipated, depressed, defeated.

"I am in the middle of a mess!" he thought, once he was alone. "I'm such a dumb ass. Now, when all had been finally forgotten . . . I'm the one who brought it all back. Yes, I am such a dumb ass! What should I do now? Tell the truth? No, I can't. No, no. Should I blame my uncle for having the pin? How will anyone find out I'm lying? Even if they see that I have the pin now, I'll say that I was in Madrid then and that I don't remember anything. That's right. Nothing. I won't cave in. My uncle is dead; who'll find out I'm not telling the truth? No one will. Perfect! And, what was all that about Egurmendi's servant trying to steal the pin from me? He sure knew what he was doing. Egurmendi must've sent him, of course. What are they plotting this time? Today I lied to Garaidi but I must help him somehow, yes, I must."

"Hello! Hello, my friend. Are you coming?"

What a scare! It was Larrola, the doctor. He opened the door suddenly and he burst into Muñube's room, yelling. After getting such astounding news from Garaidi, he'd forgotten he was expecting Larrola's visit. What a scare!

"My God!" exclaimed the newcomer. "What

happened to your eye? Have you been in a fight?"

"Yes, with a thief."

"With a thief? He sure beat you up. Did you catch him?"

"No."

"He ran away, eh? Damn!"

"Yes. It was Egurmendi's former servant."

"Egurmendi's?" said Larrola, worried. He hadn't slept after what he witnessed in the graveyard. "Egurmendi, who just passed away?"

"Yes, his servant. Do you know him?"

"No, no, but . . . No, no."

How could he conceal what he knew?

"They're despicable people," said Muñube.

Larrola wanted to help Garaidi; and, hoping that Muñube would tell him something, he asked:

"Despicable? What do you mean?"

"You don't know much about this town, but a few years ago a man disappeared because of the Egurmendis."

"A man or a woman?" he asked, remembering that he saw a woman's body in the grave.

"No, no, a man. He was a member of the Pagodi family. That's what my uncle told me on his deathbed," he said, trying to stir up Larrola's feelings. But he decided not to push it.

How was he going to tell Larrola that the thief was after Pagodi's pin, which he happened to have in his possession? They were friends, but not so close as to share that piece of information.

"Why don't you talk to the police?" said Larrola. "I know that the private investigator, with whom you saw me two nights ago, could be of great help. Apparently, he's very good."

"Garaidi? He just left."

"Really? You called him? Did you tell him anything about this story?"

"Yes, everything."

"Then, he must've told you, of course, about what we saw in Egurmendi's mausoleum," he blurted out.

"What we saw in the mausoleum!" repeated Muñube to himself. "What is this story that he seems to know and I know nothing about?"

On the one hand, if he said yes, Larrola would assume he knew everything and then wouldn't share any additional information. On the other hand, if he said no, he would stop cold and wouldn't say anything, either. So, cunningly, he decided to go halfway.

"Well, yes and no . . ."

"Well, you know . . ." began Larrola foolishly, under the impression that Muñube knew more about it than he himself. "Egurmendi's wife has a bullet hole in her forehead. Someone shot her! I'm sure of it. I saw it with my very own eyes."

Muñube looked pitiful. Once again he blushed, turned pale, blue, yellow . . . He began shivering; he was awestruck. He was completely devastated by what he just heard, so shaken that his legs couldn't hold him.

"Killed by a gunshot?" echoed Muñube.

"What do you mean? You didn't know?" began Larrola, now getting nervous.

"Me?"

Larrola realized the magnitude of what he just did.

"Oh no, what did I do?" he thought, feeling mortified, wishing he could reel back what he had just said. But once the barrel is open, the cider comes out. Muñube grabbed his coat and took off at once, shutting the door behind him as he left.

Larrola was alone once again; he didn't know what to do next. He was on the edge of losing it. He asked Muñube where he was going but he didn't get an answer. He broke the promise he made to Garaidi.

"This is bad, I'm ashamed of myself," he said covering his face with his hands. He did not react for a moment, but quickly stood up and headed to the door. It was too late. Only God knew where Muñube was by then. It was easier to play drums on an egg yolk than to catch him now.

He regretted not having followed Muñube. What was that testy man going to do next?

With nothing left to do in Muñube's bedroom, he went downstairs quietly and, without uttering a word to anyone, he headed home in despair.

He had not been able to sleep much the previous night and, with his head pounding with remorse, he would not be able to sleep much tonight, either. It was eleven at night. Where would he look for Muñube at that hour? Who knew where he was by now?

"If someone comes asking for me," he told his mother when he got home, "whoever it is, tell them that I'm out visiting a patient, that I'm in Donostia, that I'm dead; tell them whatever you want so they leave me alone. I'm not having dinner tonight. I'm going straight to bed. Good night. See you tomorrow."

"You'll get sick if you keep working so hard."

He went straight to bed and kept turning his wheels while lying restlessly. He was still at it at three in the morning.

He gave his word and yet he did not keep the secret. It was embarrassing.

# 12

# Sunday: Muñube on the Run?

The next morning, like every Sunday, Garaidi attended nine o'clock mass. Little did he know, while walking back home, that his old friend Patxi from Bilbao had come to visit him. As soon as he opened the door, his wife ran to him excitedly:

"Martin, guess who's here to see you!"

"My friend, have you been waiting long?" he greeted the visitor, happy to see him.

They were childhood friends and classmates all the way through school. They kept in touch despite one living in Bilbao and the other in Donostia. Both were in the same line of work and had often collaborated on cases.

Patxi read Garaidi's face and guessed what he was thinking.

"You didn't expect me, eh?" said Patxi. His friend was a short, husky and pleasant-looking man. From his red cheeks, one could think he was a drinker, but he was not.

"To tell you the truth, no, I didn't expect you," answered Garaidi, smiling. "I was waiting to receive the letter you promised me."

"Oh, well, I didn't have anything going on yesterday afternoon and, since today is Sunday . . . I decided to come to see you rather than mailing you a report of my findings. I caught the last train and arrived last night. I stayed at my parents' over night."

"This is perfect timing. I need your help. I am trying to solve a case."

"Martin, before you two start talking and I forget . . ." interrupted Itziar.

"Someone named Joxe Jokin from Urgain phoned asking for you. When I informed him that you weren't home he said, as soon as you got back, to tell you this: that guy you know, Muñube, who lives at the inn, hasn't been seen since last night and no one knows his whereabouts."

"When did he call?"

"About ten."

"Would you like to tag along with me?" Garaidi asked Patxi.

He didn't have to wait long for a response. They had a light mid-morning snack and were promptly on their way to Urgain. It was a wonderful day for a drive. The roadway was beautiful, but they had too much to discuss to enjoy the lovely scenery.

"So, what can you tell me about that Pirmin

fellow?" asked Garaidi, while thundering down the road.

"Elurzabal? He is very well known in Bilbao. He is originally from Navarre and lived a long time in Urgain. He's lived in Bilbao for a number of years now and has amassed a small fortune by hard work. Since arriving in Bilbao, he got married and has three young children; the oldest one about eight or ten."

"And?" interrupted Garaidi, hinting he was interested in another type of information.

"Everywhere I asked about his life," he resumed, recognizing Garaidi's inquisitiveness, "I heard nothing bad about him. I found out, through a banker friend of mine, that he is an honest man in all his dealings. I wasn't sure what you wanted to know and why, so I haven't dug up anything else. How was I going to keep snooping around without knowing exactly what you were looking for? He returned from Urgain yesterday morning."

"Yes, I know that. He left the day before yesterday."

"Are you following him?"

"Yes and no. Have you found out if he stays in touch with anyone from Urgain?"

"I'm not sure if he still does or not, but I was told that, when he first arrived in Bilbao, a gentleman from Urgain helped him negotiate the tangle of city life. Apparently, this person not only gave him a significant sum of his own money, but also put in a good word for him with the bank so he could get a loan."

"Have you found out who the Urgain benefactor was?"

"Wait, I have it written down right here," he said, pulling a piece of paper from his pocket. "Here it is. Egurmendi . . ."

"It had to be!"

"What's going on here? C'mon, you better come clean. It's about time you let me in on this," exploded Patxi, finally.

And little by little, calmly and carefully, by the time they arrived in Urgain, Garaidi had summarized everything. But he left out his doubts, gut feelings and suspicions so as not to influence Patxi's opinion. Stating the unvarnished facts would allow Patxi to take a different line on the case and, maybe, help Garaidi unravel the knot. He could develop theories that Garaidi had overlooked. They might identify new avenues of information.

That was exactly what Garaidi was after. He wanted to keep his impressions, good or bad, to himself, listen to Patxi's ideas, right or wrong, and after considering everything, reveal the truth.

"Now, I would like you to know the latest developments of this messy case. So let's get to it," he said while finally parking his car in front of Joxe Jokin's inn. Do you see that old man standing next to the door? That's Joxe Jokin. He'll really clean out your ears. Just wait!"

"He doesn't look bad."

They got out of the car.

"Hello, Joxe Jokin! Good morning! Enjoying the sun, eh?"

"Good morning to you too. I was watching, wondering if you'd come."

"This is a good friend of mine, here to assist me. You can speak freely in front of him," said Garaidi, when he noticed Joxe Jokin looking at Patxi from the corner of his eyes.

"Let's go upstairs, let's go!" the old man said anxiously.

They entered the inn.

"Bixenta!" yelled Joxe Jokin on their way upstairs, "bring something for these fellows."

"Gentlemen, gentlemen, I don't know . . ." said Joxe Jokin nervously, shuffling his feet and leading the way upstairs.

They entered the same room where Garaidi and Joxe Jokin had been the other day. As soon as Bixenta placed a pitcher full of sweet wine and a few soft rolls on the table, Joxe Jokin sat down, unable to hold it in any longer and without giving his guests a chance to utter a word, he erupted:

"Did your wife tell you I called you earlier? We've lost Muñube! I'm not sure what, but something has happened to him. He hasn't been here since last night. He hasn't slept here! I know from my daughter that you were here last night. After you left, another friend of his came to see him. I know, because I saw him go upstairs with my own eyes. But then, I completely forgot about them. I can't always be on top of everything that happens at the inn. But, nevertheless, hours passed and it got quite late with no Muñube in sight. I asked Bixenta to fetch him from his room because his dinner was getting cold. She went upstairs and returned shortly saying that there was nobody in his room. What a predicament! I went upstairs and . . . it was true, all his things were there but no trace of Muñube or his friend. I don't know how they left without being seen. They vanished like ghosts. Since then, we haven't heard from him."

"He must've gone somewhere else to have dinner with his friend," said Patxi.

"To have dinner, you say? No sir, no. He used to be something of a birdbrain but he's straightened up. Muñube seldom skips a meal at the inn. Whenever he has missed one, he has let us know ahead of time. And what about not showing up to sleep? Jesu-u-u-us! Not to come to sleep! That's a first. Never before. Something must've happened to him. Maybe he got hit by a train, or maybe he drowned, or he was struck by lightning and dropped stone-dead right there."

"Don't get carried away, Joxe Jokin. Didn't they leave together?"

"What do I know! No one saw them leave."

"Have you seen his friend since?"

"Me? No. This damn leg of mine makes moving around hard. But, I sent my daughter to his house looking for him. Wait a minute . . ."

He walked to the door and, yelling over and over, called his daughter. She was upstairs at once.

"Manuela, tell these gentlemen what they told you," Joxe Jokin directed her.

'That he wasn't at home."

"That's it," her father cut in while pacing the room. "He wasn't home."

"He didn't go home all night, either?" asked Garaidi.

"You said, dinner?" asked Joxe Jokin, holding his hand behind his ear, open mouthed and wrinkling his nose.

"No. I asked if his friend didn't go home all night, either," replied Garaidi, half shouting.

"Yes, yes," continued Joxe Jokin, not letting his daughter get a word in. "He slept at home but when she went looking for him, he had gone to visit a patient. Isn't that right? O.K., O.K. Tell these gentlemen . . . O.K. What else?" He was restless and unable to remain quiet.

"Nothing else," answered his daughter, sounding foolish.

The other two could hardly hide their smiles. It was such a hilarious scene.

"That's right, nothing else," Joxe Jokin echoed. "He slept there but was gone when she went . . .

too bad . . . Manuela, you can leave now."

She didn't need to be told twice. Without saying a word, she left the same way she came.

"So, Muñube's friend is a doctor?" asked Garaidi.

"Yes."

"Larrola?"

"Yes! Do you know him?" he asked, placing his hand, like always, behind his ear and looking at Garaidi sideways.

"Not really, but . . . I know that he is Muñube's friend."

"I don't know, but with Friday's fight and now Muñube's escape, I'm really dizzy. That is why I called you. Rest-assured that I haven't said anything to anyone. I kept it quiet. All this might be terrible for business."

"Don't worry. He'll be back in no time. Don't panic."

But poor Joxe Jokin was worried.

Garaidi had asked him not to tell anything to anyone, so he spent all day by himself to avoid the urge to tell anyone about it. It was very hard for him to stay quiet and this effort almost made him sick. On top of that, now Muñube had fled. Was he supposed to keep this to himself too? He was terrified and ready to burst.

They finally calmed him down.

Suddenly Garaidi rose to his feet and said:

"Let's go pay a visit to this doctor."

"Do you know where he lives? My daughter will accompany you."

"No, no, thank you. I know where it is."

Joxe Jokin, scratching the back of his ear, wondered:

"How does he know about the doctor? He must be working on something I don't know."

"If you find out anything else, Joxe Jokin, call me at Herriburu's house. We'll be there soon. And . . . I hope you cheer up!"

"Cheer up amid all these problems? Easy for you to say!"

13

# So Many Lies

They found Larrola at home. The person at the door said that he just got in and intended to leave right away.

Larrola came at once, elegantly dressed, pretending to be glad to see them, when it was obvious he was reluctant to meet Garaidi face to face. His eyes said it all. Unlike three days earlier when he acted pompously, this morning Larrola looked quite sheepish. He kept his turmoil bottled up. He invited them to his office. It looked well equipped. In a corner a few leather chairs and a nice table; on the other side there was a shiny metal exam table covered with a white sheet; next to it, a white shelf full of medical tools; the smell of medicine was overwhelming.

After some small talk they asked him about Muñube . . . he hadn't seen him all morning; he didn't know anything . . . as if dancing around the subject . . .

"Last night you were with Muñube at Joxe Jokin's inn," began Garaidi. "Did you leave together?"

He did not have to lie about that so he replied angrily and firmly that they did not.

"Did he tell you where he was headed?"

"No, he didn't."

That was exactly what Larrola wanted to know, too, where Muñube was. That was all he could think the whole night. How could he get rid of that nagging worry, eating at him like a parasite?

"As far as we know, he hasn't slept at the inn," said Garaidi.

Larrola felt uneasy after his conversation with Muñube the night before; he still felt uneasy. He knew that Joxe Jokin's daughter had asked about Muñube, too. And that damn Muñube had vanished without saying a word or leaving a trace. Everyone was looking for Muñube. How could he not worry?

"Will he be at his parents'?" they asked him.

"I don't know," he lied.

Didn't he just return from there after learning he was not at his parents' house?

"Will he be with his girlfriend?"

"He might," he lied again.

Joxe Jokin was worried; Larrola worried even more. How could he have broken his word and told Muñube about what he saw at the grave?

How could he tell them now that Muñube bolted as soon as he heard about it? He could not.

Larrola was distressed but he tried hard to appear calm.

He kept asking himself, "Where the devil did that knuckle-head go? Why are they looking for him? What's the connection between Muñube and that gravesite? He acted astounded when he found out about it. He took off so suddenly, that jackass. And now what?"

This was not a matter of small change. Garaidi was looking for Muñube. One would think that Muñube had shot that woman.

He sweated while they poked and prodded, trying to make him spill everything he knew.

But let's continue following these players.

"Those were empty excuses," said Patxi when they left the house. "He's not trustworthy. If we had pushed him a little more, pressured him more. . . He's keeping something. He didn't tell us the whole story."

"I agree, but why push him harder now? We'll get to him later."

"What's your plan?"

"We must find Muñube soon and watch Egurmendi and Elurzabal closely."

"You have them both in your pocket."

"Not in my pocket but under surveillance."

"You must have quite a set of eyes," said Patxi with a grin, mocking Garaidi by looking furtively from side to side as they spoke.

"Yes, Patxi. I have two people following them. What time is it?"

"Twelve-twenty."

"Let's go toward the church before people get out of the twelve o'clock mass."

"What for?"

"Maritxu told me that Egurmendi usually attends that mass and I believe that we should keep an eye on him. Of course, Joxe Ramon, my man, will be there, watching him closely, too.

"Let's not waste any time, then."

14

# Watching Egurmendi

They arrived at the right time, at the perfect time. People had just begun coming out of the church. First, a bunch of young boys, running, skipping, and yelling as they left the church, took to the streets; next, clusters of people; then, a stream; and, at last, only a few left.

Some of the churchgoers, most of them actually, as soon as they were outside, left immediately for home or for a stroll, enjoying the sunshine. They were gone quickly. It was a beautiful day. Others stayed in small huddles, conversing at the church doorsteps, and a few remained by themselves as if waiting, one for a girlfriend, another his wife or, still others, their friends.

Eventually, Egurmendi appeared. Garaidi elbowed his friend to signal the arrival. He was smartly dressed, all in black. Garaidi's man was there, too, following Egurmendi closely. His trained eyes immediately spotted Garaidi and

Patxi. He approached them.

"Good morning gentlemen. Nice to see you again," he said as he shook Patxi's hand. Then he looked at Garaidi and asked, "Have you seen our worm?"

He was referring to Egurmendi. Joxe Ramon called everyone who he had to watch under Garaidi's orders, 'worm.'

"Any news?" asked Garaidi.

"Nothing new. He stayed at home before mass. Some people came over to pay their respects, but I didn't sense anything suspicious. On his way to church he went in and out of that elegant inn on Main Street. I couldn't hear what he said but he exchanged a few words with a woman at the door. He didn't look very happy. Other than that . . . I'm getting hungry . . ."

"Joxe Ramon, you can leave. We'll follow him from here. I asked Justino to come by Egurmendi's house at two o'clock. You come back at midnight and you better have slept!"

"Of course I'll have slept."

"Do you know someone named Muñube?"

"Muñube? Not me. A new worm?"

"You'll need to know him. When you come to relieve Justino at midnight, he'll give you a photo of him. Call me as soon as you see him."

"Bye now, boss! Keep your eyes peeled and don't let the worm get away."

Meanwhile, Mr. Egurmendi was in front of

the church, apparently not at all worried. From time to time, he glanced toward the church door; obviously waiting for someone. Five or six men walked up to him individually to express their condolences, he shook their hands and, after exchanging a few words, they left. His late father had so many friends.

By then most people had left church with the exception of an elderly woman or two. Egurmendi must have realized that the person he was looking for had not attended mass or perhaps he got tired of waiting. For one reason or another, he set off down the street alone. Little did he know that our two friends were close behind him.

He was walking the streets, headed straight to his fiancée's house. She lived on one of the most beautiful streets in Urgain. The house was gorgeous, too: three stories, white, spotless.

He arrived at Karmentxu's doorstep, rang the bell twice, as he always did, and waited. That was a familiar code for Karmentxo.

Our two friends saw a bar right across the street and, deciding that they could watch the house from there without being noticed, went inside.

Egurmendi was looking left and right, pacing back and forth from one side of the house to the other. He would stop for a bit once he reached one side and then he would walk back to the other side, looking occasionally at the house. It was obvious that he was waiting for his fiancée to come down to meet him.

In the meantime, Garaidi and Patxi were sitting comfortably at a table by the bar entrance, drinking some wine. Although their eyes were fixed on Karmentxo's house, no one would guess they were following Egurmendi.

Fifteen minutes later, they were still watching Egurmendi from the bar. He looked uneasy; checked his watch; he would occasionally get close to the door to listen for footsteps; he would stop, take a few steps, look over his shoulder and continue pacing back and forth.

Finally, after looking at the upstairs windows a hundred times, Egurmendi entered the building. He seemed quite angry. The other two kept their eyes glued to the entrance. After five minutes, at most, Egurmendi was back on the street alone again, downcast and frowning. Without stopping, he left on foot, his head bowed.

"Follow him," Garaidi told his friend. "I'll stay here. We'll meet later somewhere in front of his house or in Herriburu's house. Quick, go after him."

Patxi was behind Egurmendi in an instant. Garaidi, on the other hand, paid their tab at the bar and promptly entered Karmentxo's house. He knew from Maritxu that she lived on the first floor. He was a master at improvising excuses. Yes, indeed. As on other occasions, he hoped he would have some inspiration when the door opened and, without thinking twice, he knocked. *Danba*! No one answered the first time, nor the second or the third.

Probably due to the noise he made, the second floor neighbor, a small-waisted, long-legged woman with disheveled hair, who resembled a witch, appeared and asked:

"Are you looking for Amunda?"

"Yes, ma'am. They aren't home?"

"I don't think so and it's strange. I just told Mr. Egurmendi the same thing. They were home yesterday afternoon, but I haven't seen them today. Their windows are shut tight. They never leave their house. I don't know where they could've gone. Do you want me to tell them anything when they get back?"

"No, no thank you. It doesn't matter."

Maritxu had told him that Karmentxo lived with her parents who were not that old but were sickly, especially her mother. How could they all be out, then? Shocking. They left without telling anyone anything? If Egurmendi had known about it, he wouldn't have waited for her as long as he did.

Who knew what happened there? What if the mother suddenly got worse and they took her to a hospital? Were they on the run, perhaps? It was hard to know. So many things could've happened. In any case, the windows were closed tight; it looked like no one lived there.

"When do you think they left?" Garaidi asked her.

"How would I know? Last night, this morning maybe? I don't know. I haven't seen them since yesterday afternoon."

"And you didn't hear them leave?"

"I'm telling you. Nothing, nothing at all. If I had heard something . . ." she said rolling her eyes. Garaidi could guess what she wasn't telling him . . . 'If I'd heard something, I would've been here peeking through the door crack.' "No I didn't hear anything."

Garaidi believed her; yes, he did.

# 15

# In Front of His House. . .

Egurmendi's mansion (what a beautiful house!) was located on top of a mound surrounded by a field of lilacs. There were many beautiful mansions and gardens in Urgain, each more beautiful than the next, but very few were as beautiful as this one.

Garaidi had seen them all and had stopped more than once at this one and wondered to whom the house belonged. How could he have known that, eventually, he would be investigating its owner? Who would've thought? Nevertheless, "was Egurmendi capable of killing his wife?" he asked himself. It was hard to believe but for now, he couldn't shake off that suspicion.

The entrance to Egurmendi's garden, like many other mansions in Urgain, went through an elm grove, and that was quite a grove. Children and the elderly . . . someone could always be found sitting on the stone benches when the weather was nice, especially on holidays around midday.

On this beautiful, early Sunday afternoon, Garaidi came from Amunda's house straight to the grove where most benches were already taken. Patxi was there too, alone, reading the newspaper, at least pretending to, sitting like a baron.

Garaidi walked up to him.

"Anything?" he asked as he sat back to back without looking at him.

"He came straight home and nothing has happened since then. He's still inside. And you?" he asked without lifting his eyes from the newspaper.

"There's no one in Karmentxo's home. That is why he looked so dejected. I found out from a busybody neighbor that no one has seen them since yesterday afternoon."

"She doesn't know where they went?"

"No. She is quite puzzled, too. Apparently, Karmentxo's mother is quite sickly. I can't believe that the neighbor hasn't followed them, flying on her broom."

"First Muñube disappears," said Patxi as if he were talking to himself, "and now Karmentxo and her parents. Are these knots made out of the same thread?"

"I would say so."

Both remained silent; one unaware if he were holding his newspaper upright or upside down; the other looking at children playing on the next bench.

"Here comes Justino," said Garaidi.

It looked like no one was at Egurmendi's house, but who knew if they were peeking from some hidden place.

"Do you have a new man?" asked Patxi, pretending to read the newspaper, but looking sideways.

"Yes, and he seems smart."

He was wandering about while rolling a cigarette. As soon as he saw Garaidi he approached him.

"Excuse me, sir," he said when he was next to him. "Do you have a light?" He sneered, looking at Patxi, wanting to know who this man was.

"Good morning, Justino," replied Garaidi while trying to find a match in his pocket. "Don't worry, this man behind me is a good friend of mine. Egurmendi is at home. We're leaving now so you watch him. One of us will be back before dusk. Joxe Ramon will be here by twelve. See you later."

In the meantime, he lit his cigarette. He thanked Garaidi and, as calm as when he approached him, walked to another bench and sat down.

Without having listened to this conversation, even if Egurmendi himself were lurking nearby, no one would have guessed that these three gentlemen were working together. Certainly, those carefree strollers in the garden (not a small number, by the way) had no idea.

After a short while, since it was lunchtime, they headed to Herriburu's house, first Garaidi, then Patxi a bit later. They were starving.

"First things first, my friend."

16

# Joxe Jokin the Detective

Meanwhile in Joxe Jokin's nice dining room, with which we are now familiar, Joxe Jokin reads the newspaper and, why not just say it, he is grousing because there is no news about Muñube. There are no other guests in the dining room yet.
Let's listen.

A poised server is on her way, bringing a steamy pot of stew for the delight of noses!

"Good day, sir."

". . . Um!"

"Here's some stew."

". . . Ummm!"

"Any good news, sir?"

"Nothing."

"Did you read about that poor man?"

"What poor man?"

'The one who disappeared."

"Disappeared? Who? Muñube?"

The newspaper slipped from his hands and in

an effort to catch it, he hit the ladle and knocked it to the floor. While trying to retrieve it, he lost the now sparking, half-lit pipe he was smoking. Everything was covered in embers and he burst into a coughing fit . . . finally everything returned to normal.

"Muñube?" said the server. "Muñube has disappeared?"

"No, no," he replied, irritated. "Don't you confuse me."

And quickly, dying to know more, he asked her in a nicer way, "Who do you say disappeared?"

"What do I know! It says it all there."

"I haven't seen anything. And where did you say he disappeared?" he asked while examining the newspaper.

"Here, in Urgain."

"In Urgain? And where did it say that?"

She kept looking for that news here and there over Joxe Jokin's shoulder, but it was no use.

"You've dreamed it, girl."

"No, sir, no. It was a full page, pictures and all."

"Then, where is it?"

"I don't think it was the same newspaper," she said when she looked at the paper closely.

"Was it perhaps in last night's? Go and look for it. See if they haven't burnt it in the stove yet. It wouldn't surprise me. Go, go now!"

She was back right away, holding last night's

paper. It was missing a few pages and it didn't look all that clean, but they couldn't find it there, either. Perusing it forward and backward, grease stains and all, the news Joxepa Antoni mentioned was nowhere to be found.

"You all are going to drive me crazy!" said Joxe Jokin, aggravated. "There's nothing here. There's nothing here!"

"But I saw it!"

"You dumb girl! Sure, you saw it, in bed, in your dreams!"

"On the bed! That's it!" she hollered. "Mr. Muñube had a magazine on his bed. Yes! Right there. This morning when I was cleaning the room . . . It was right there!"

She was feeling absolutely over the moon. She was ecstatic. To tell the truth, it is easy for small minds to overflow.

"Go get it for me. Quick, go!"

She brought him a couple wrinkled newspapers. They looked yellowish, like Joxe Jokin's skin.

"Oh, now!" he began, infuriated, as soon as he saw them. "These are from twenty years ago! Child! Leave me alone and get back to work. Shoo! Get out! Go away!"

Joxepa Antoni shrank away meekly. Joxe Jokin, realizing that his stew had gotten cold, began shoveling it down, grumbling. The wrinkled newspapers remained on the table, right next to him.

He wasn't finished eating, but his curiosity drove him to look at the paper once every two spoonfuls, then twice between spoonfuls, then he began to read this, later to read that . . . And of course, Urgain, Pagodi, Egurmendi, all those names and stories with which he was familiar began coming up.

Without stopping to eat, he resembled an old rooster looking for worms in loose soil, turning his head to one side, then to the next, not letting any go. And suddenly, he unearthed a huge worm: Pagodi's lapel pin!

Somehow, he shoved the piece of bread he held in his hand into his mouth; held the newspaper with both hands and did not say a word, surprisingly, until he reached the very last period; such was his curiosity.

Joxe Jokin was not only an expert at talking but he was no amateur at identifying and fixing snags, either. Show him a ball and question whether it was round? Good luck! Pay him with counterfeit money? No way! Lose his way on the streets of 'his' Buenos Aires? Never!

He was a non-stop, one-way conversation, a champion gossip, a singular chatterbox. Anything from old wives tales, to stories about gamblers, the Cuban war, rowing championships, stories about his American adventures, blacks and whites, the powerful and the weak, the big and the small, the righteous and the sinners, what is, was and will be, on any topic, he would have a comment for you. The fact that his tongue kept at it did not mean his eyes and ears rested. Although he had carried it on his shoulders for many years, his head was still sharp.

He guessed that the pin in Muñube's possession belonged to Pagodi. He was such an old bloodhound.

He had often seen those papers and had held that pin in his hands countless times but, like he said, who would've thought that the pin belonged to Pagodi?

Quietly, without talking to anyone, all alone, he dragged himself up to Muñube's room; slowly he opened the door; haltingly opened the small wooden box and . . . what? The pin was gone! Good God!

Frowning once again, he returned to the dining room. After cramming those wrinkled clippings into his pocket, he called his daughter. He was already worried about Muñube's escape and this new finding did not calm him down any.

His daughter came and stood behind him. "Do you have any news about Muñube?" he asked her quietly, so customers sitting at other tables would not hear.

"No."

"Where is that scoundrel? Hell!"

His daughter stood behind him, staring.

"Manuela!"

Manuela remained quietly behind him.

"Manuela!" As soon as he realized she was behind him, he said: "Here you are. Are Muñube's things in his room?"

"Well . . ."

"No one has stolen anything, eh?"

"Hm . . ."

"No one has entered his room except the maid, right?

"Hm . . ."

"No one has touched the money, eh?

"Hm . . ."

"Do you remember the lapel pin that Muñube kept in that small box on the shelf?"

". . ."

"It's gone."

"Hm . . ."

Joxe Jokin knew that the last "hm . . ." meant "perhaps."

"Yes, yes! . . . Of course! . . .You can go now. Go, go! . . ."

He sent his daughter off and waved her goodbye. She looked exhausted after so much chatting and a little perplexed because she was no dummy. But she had so much work on her plate. "Heck with men. They can fix it on their own. Muñube . . . What a dimwit!"

Joxe Jokin stood up and, without finishing his lunch, left for his room muttering, "Unbelievable! Muñube had Pagodi's pin. Crazy! Pirmin trying to steal it and now Muñube's flight. This could ruin my inn!" He mumbled under his breath.

Once he was in his room, he called for his daughter and handed her a sealed letter, telling her dryly, "This has been a terrible night, daughter. I'm not feeling well and I'm going to bed. Take this letter and keep it until Mr. Garaidi comes. It's for him. Don't you lose it. And, do not say a word, not a peep."

His daughter did not even ask him what was the matter and why she should keep quiet. Telling her to keep quiet was like telling a rock to stay put.

17

# What to Do Next?

"Right. We've hardly cast any light on what we found in the grave," said Garaidi, sitting at the Herriburu's table after swallowing another tasty piece of salmon that Maritxu had prepared, while the host couple and Patxi listened. "Truly, we've hardly made any progress on that discovery because we didn't want to incriminate any innocent people due to our lack of knowledge in the case. Besides, your wife is so sure that Egurmendi is innocent."

"Yes, Martin, yes," added Herriburu as he kept eating. "I've told you before. I've known Egurmendi very well for a long time, and I can't believe that he has committed such a senseless act."

Herriburu, who had returned home that morning, was a good, but hot-tempered, man. His wife had made him rush back home, shouting and lamenting over the phone about the terrible things that had happened and how much she needed him.

They all knew each other already and after greeting one another, they began conversing agreeably. Garaidi and Patxi were happy to have found Herriburu at home.

"That's why," said Garaidi, after Herriburu's honest, nosy and know-it-all maid Joxepa, whom we have already met, made a round trip from the kitchen, "that is precisely why we are conducting our investigation with maximum discretion, to keep from harming Egurmendi's good name. But now we have another problem.

Husband and wife stopped eating and concentrated their attention on him.

"I've heard from Muñube about some kind of a dispute between Egurmendi and Pagodi."

"Muñube? The old doctor's nephew?" asked Herriburu, listening closely.

"That's the one."

"And what does that moron have to say?"

"He claims that, apparently, his uncle told him on his deathbed that Egurmendi was responsible for everything that happened to Pagodi."

"What a thing to say! Egurmendi! Hear that, Maritxu? Egurmendi! Ha, ha, ha . . . I have never heard anything so amusing. Egurmendi!" burst Herriburu.

And then, infuriated, he said:

"I don't believe it! No way. Do you hear me? No way! Those were nothing but his uncle's deathbed delusions. Nothing more. Delusions! How could Egurmendi bring himself to harm Pagodi? They were best friends. C'mon. How could you even consider it? It's nothing but nonsense."

"Muñube knows something about Pagodi."

"Muñube? That lazy bum can't know much. He's only good for living off someone else's work. As river water runs downstream, that's how he runs to laziness," said Herriburu, aggressively and exorbitantly. "Besides, what's the connection between this and what was found inside the casket?"

"Hold on," replied, Patxi trying to calm Herriburu down. "Martin and I believe that clearing up this story also will help us solve the other one you mention."

"I don't see how they can be connected," he snorted. "After all this time, who knows what happened to Pagodi? You're twenty years too late, don't you think?"

"You're right, we don't know yet what happened to him," Garaidi interrupted. "But, we found something he had in his possession when he disappeared."

"Really? And what is that?" asked Maritxu in lively curiosity.

"This, right here," and he showed her Pagodi's lapel pin. "This is the pin that Pagodi was wearing when he disappeared."

"What a presumption! How do you know that?" Herriburu interrupted him as he had earlier.

"It's a long story, but rest assured, it's true. Look at his engraved initials on the inside."

"And where did you find it?" he asked, not wanting to take it into consideration, but examining the pin carefully.

"Muñube himself had it."

"Muñube?" the couple asked in surprised unison.

"Amazing, huh? You should also know that a former servant of Egurmendi tried to steal this same pin from Muñube the day before yesterday, and that, since yesterday, no one knows of Muñube's whereabouts."

"Wait, wait," said Patxi, noticing them going into a daze.

"Do you know Karmentxo, Egurmendi's fiancée?" began Garaidi once again. "Well, she and her parents are gone too."

"But her mother has been feeling very ill lately," interjected Maritxu.

Herriburu looked astounded, listening to Garaidi, but soon recovered his obstinacy and said:

"I doubt that what you have said so far is relevant at all," he began. "Muñube, that stupid idiot must be somewhere loafing as usual. He'll turn up if he wants to. Otherwise, he can remain wherever he is. On the other hand, the Amundas most likely have gone to visit some relative, or they must've had to go somewhere."

"And Egurmendi didn't know?"

"And who told you he didn't know?"

"He didn't know."

They told him everything we already know; that they followed him after mass; that he kept waiting for his fiancée for a long time; what the upstairs neighbor with tangled, greasy hair had told them; this and that . . . they told him everything.

"And what do you think?" asked Herriburu, beginning to believe that there could be some truth to what they were saying.

"What Patxi has already told you," replied Garaidi, "that finding out what happened to Pagodi will help us shed light on the graveyard mystery. In other words: this knot will lead us to the other knot's loose end."

"So? What's your plan?"

"We must find Pagodi, alive or dead."

"It's not an easy task. Where are you going to start from?"

"From right here!" replied Garaidi, displaying the pin.

That seemed like a good starting point.

"I wonder how Muñube obtained that pin," interjected Maritxu.

"He says that his uncle gave it to him. Was he an honest man?"

"Aw, he was a little strange," replied Herriburu, full of contempt.

"And how did he get it?" asked Maritxu again.

"It's all a lie! Cheap talk!" said Herriburu, exposing his bad temper. "That freeloader took advantage of his uncle until his death. Those were the days he was spoiled rotten. But once he began working . . ."

"You are too harsh with poor Muñube," Maritxu scolded him. "What do you have against him?"

"What a thing to say! Really? Me, harsh! I am not the villain here. I'm not the one blaming Egurmendi for what happened to Pagodi. The pin is in his possession and you say I'm harsh? C'mon! What do you want me to do, sing his praises?"

Yes, he was furious. Truth be told, who was Muñube, that lazy bum, to accuse the most upstanding man in town of foul play?

He couldn't believe what they found at the grave to be true. Nevertheless, how could all of them have seen wrong? What if they were right? But no matter what Garaidi had seen or said, it was impossible. How could Egurmendi's wife have a bullet hole in her forehead? Impossible, indeed.

And now, what should he do? Tell the police? The news would petrify the whole town. It would cause a thousand tongues to wag.

Herriburu was fond of the truth and wanted to bring it to light but, on one hand, due to his bond of friendship with Egurmendi, and on the other, due to his belief in Egurmendi's innocence, he wanted all investigations to be conducted in complete secrecy. But . . . what should they do next?

They spent hours sharing opinions, considering each other's assumptions and clarifying ideas without reaching a consensus. Finally, the four of them decided to leave the matter in Garaidi's hands. He knew best what needed to be done.

And his final decision, for now anyway, was, to shut up. He would continue investigating and . . .

"That's it, Martin," Herriburu interrupted him. "I'm with you. Keeping this mess to ourselves is the best we can do for Egurmendi."

"But what if he ends up being guilty?" said Maritxu fearfully.

"What if he ends up being guilty, you say?" her husband interrupted grumbling at her, showing his sharp edge. "Then we'll tell the police. Simple! But for now, let's keep working discretely. Let's hope I am not mistaken. Watch out Muñube! You liar, you lazy slug!"

It was about four when Garaidi and Patxi left; one headed to Donostia and the other to the grounds of Egurmendi's house.

18

# Crooked Muñube. . .

Sraight from Urgain, Garaidi arrives at Muñube's girlfriend's front door in Donostia.

"Excuse me, ma'am," Garaidi addressed a good-looking woman that came to open the door. "Is Mr. Muñube in?"

"Muñube? No. He doesn't live here."

"Yes, I know he doesn't live here, but . . ."

"Yes, he's Begoña's boyfriend, but he hasn't set foot here. Begoña left to meet him, so they must be together."

"Where will they be?"

"God knows! They won't be back until nine at the earliest. What do you want me to tell them?"

"Nothing. Don't bother."

He was looking for an excuse and said:

"I'm Muñube's friend," he lied. "I want to return this pin that he lent me. But, it's not a big deal, I'll give it to him tomorrow." And, with that, he showed her Pagodi's lapel pin.

It just took a moment, one peek. Little did Garaidi suspect that showing the pin would tighten up Pagodi's already tightly-twisted knot even more.

As soon as the woman saw the pin, she said:

"Hey, that's Begoña's pin!"

Garaidi's jaw dropped. "Begoña's pin?" He did not expect to hear that. How could that be?

He composed himself and, before she could sense his astonishment, said:

"How can this be Begoña's pin? It was Muñube who lent it to me."

"Sure. That's because Begoña gave it to him."

"Are you sure?"

"Yes, sir, I'm sure. She inherited it from her parents when they died."

"Oh, no! I didn't mean to get him in trouble. Won't Begoña get mad at him now that he has lent it to me?" added Garaidi cunningly, smiling.

She was no dimwit and she quickly guessed what he meant. She laughed and told him:

"Don't worry. She won't find out. Rest assured."

"In God's name. Please don't tell her."

Someone was coming up the stairs and they hushed, looking down the stairwell.

A beautiful, blue-eyed young woman turned up. She was coming up the stairs, light on her feet, in a hurry, looking up, but as soon as she spotted Garaidi, she looked worried. Still half-smiling, she remarked to the landlady:

"I thought it was Inaxio."

From the effort of running or the embarrassment generated from encountering Garaidi, she blushed. Garaidi was overjoyed! It was Begoña, herself. Muñube didn't have a bad eye, by God.

As soon as the landlady explained that Garaidi was a friend of Inaxio, Begoña said with alarm:

"Oh, no. What's happened to him?"

She was afraid that Garaidi bore bad news.

Garaidi tried to ease her mind tenderly, but no matter what she was told, she remained worried. Inaxio did not show up and did not even call. He never missed a date but . . . today? Did he love her or didn't he? Did he forget the date or didn't he? Did he get hurt or was he O.K.? Inaxio here, Inaxio there . . . Begoña's mind was overflowing with questions and did not pay any attention to what Garaidi had to say.

Garaidi was immersed in his thoughts, too.

It hadn't been a waste of time to come see this young woman. He caught Muñube in a lie and the game was up. Yes, sir. Why had he lied to him? Was he trying to help solve the disappearance case or was he trying to hide something? Lie after lie, what was the connection between Muñube and Pagodi's case? His hands were not clean. And, what about Begoña's parents?

As he thought before, it looked like that woman's death and Pagodi's disappearance shared a common thread. Yes, they had to be connected somehow. It was not a coincidence that those two events happened the same day. But how the devil could he connect them? This was Garaidi's dilemma.

He had two different paths to pursue in his investigation. One was to follow the ugliness from the graveyard, and the other to track Pagodi. Where could he begin looking for the woman's killer? Truly, he did not have much to go on were he to follow this path. If confronted, wouldn't Elurzabal deny everything? How could he wheedle anything from him without giving up what he knew about the early morning business and the scuffle?

He could tell him the truth, but what if he were guilty? Wouldn't he begin to deny everything? And if he were innocent, wouldn't he become incensed?

And, on the other hand, where could he begin looking for Pagodi? At least, he had a nice loose end there, his lapel pin. All he needed to do was follow the pin and Begoña's parents. In other words, he had only to chase down Muñube's lie. Where would that thread lead him?

As he considered his options, he returned home wondering if there were any news from Urgain. There was not. Nevertheless, he called Herriburu first and then Joxe Jokin's inn. Patxi answered the phone at the inn and what he told

Garaidi left him completely flabbergasted.

"Listen! Joxe Jokin fell ill and he is in bed. He left his daughter a letter for us. Listen to this. He says that the Muñube we are after is guilty, that he is nothing but an assassin. He tells us to rest assured about it, that he is certain about it . . . Catch him right away!"

Muñube, pretending he was an innocent, white dove, the one trying to correct other people's wrongdoing!

Garaidi had his suspicions but he did not think Muñube was involved this deeply. He considered: "After all, wasn't it Muñube who was in possession of Pagodi's pin? Didn't he lie to me? Wasn't he on his way back from the cemetery that night when Larrola and I were headed there? Didn't he get into a fight with Pirmin Elurzabal?"

He headed straight to Muñube's parents' house, but he was not there and his parents knew nothing of his whereabouts. Immediately, he got into his car and headed to Urgain. As soon as he arrived, he went to Joxe Jokin's bar, he sat at a table alone with a glass of wine before him and he saw Patxi, acting very calm, but . . .

As he ordered another drink, Garaidi asked him under his breath, so no one else would hear him: "Any news?"

"There was no trace of Muñube. And, based on what Joxe Jokin said, don't expect him to suddenly appear. Here is his letter."

It wasn't a very long message. Apparently Joxe Jokin's fingers were not as nimble as his tongue.

"Where did this come from?" wondered a frowning Garaidi when he finished reading.

"How would I know? I talked to him after I got the letter, but he didn't elaborate. He said that he couldn't imagine harboring a person like that in his place, but that he is certain of what he says in the letter, to make sure to catch Muñube right away, watch out . . . and that's all! I tried hard but he didn't disclose the source of his information. Didn't you tell me he's a blabbermouth?"

"Wasn't he?"

"Not today, apparently."

"He must not be feeling well. Where is he now?"

"He's asleep. He asked us to leave him alone until tomorrow. We need to wait."

"We need to wait. And besides that?"

"Besides that, not much happened in Urgain; nothing worth mentioning, anyway."

"Egurmendi hasn't left his house all afternoon. Your man is staying put. And in Donostia?" asked Patxi.

"In Donostia? If you only knew!"

Patxi was amazed after hearing what Garaidi had to say about what he learned at Begoña's. Muñube sure fooled him in no small way.

His behavior was suspicious; his lie was obvious; a cowardly flight . . . But, nevertheless, he had been the first to mention Pagodi and . . .

And Begoña? What was Begoña's involvement in all this and that of her parents? Garaidi told Patxi that in Donostia he learned little new information about Begoña from that talkative landlady: That Begoña was an orphan; French by birth; that she lived there for a long time and that she owned a charming store; that she had an elegant boyfriend (our Muñube, that is), seven dresses, five pairs of earrings, three leather purses . . .

"You're right, that's not much," interrupted Patxi, grinning. "If she owned ten pairs of earrings instead of five . . ."

"For now we'll need to settle for this . . ."

They had a lot of work ahead of them. They couldn't say that they didn't have any information at this point but, did what they have get them anywhere? They were not sure. He had to admit, they hardly had anything helpful.

For Inaxi, of course, it was obvious: Pirmin was guilty. For Maritxu, old Dr. Muñube was the guilty one. In her husband's opinion, the feather-brained younger Muñube was guilty and he did everything he could to blame it on him. Joxe Jokin, for his part, also lashed out against young Muñube.

And all of them were so sure!

What about Garaidi? What did Garaidi think? Who, in his opinion, was guilty?

Find Muñube! This was their first step; they

had to track down Muñube. There were still so many knots to undo, so much treachery to be revealed.

But until they found Muñube . . .

# 19

# Sisters? Mother and Daughter?

It was dusk. Something had to be done and, while they waited for Joxe Jokin to wake up, they decided to go to Egurmendi's house. They found a quick excuse. Hadn't he been Pagodi's friend? And hadn't Garaidi been hired to find Pagodi? It was the perfect excuse.

And, as Garaidi said:

"If nothing else, let's just harass him with this excuse."

At once, they were ringing his doorbell. His house was a mansion made out of chiseled stone and located in the middle of a fragrant flower garden. All through the grounds, clear paths made out of pebbles crisscrossed the lily garden; here, a small fountain; under pockets of shade, stone chairs and tables; all around, clusters of plants in bloom.

They did not have time to enjoy that beautiful scene. As soon as the doorbell faded, a robust man came to the door.

"I am Mr. Garaidi from Donostia," he said and handed him a business card. "We would like to talk with Mr. Egurmendi."

He had them come in the house at once.

Inside the house, everything was beautiful, too. It was obvious that the Egurmendi family was rich. If the entrance looked like this, what would the main rooms look like?

He showed them to a big room before he left to summon the homeowner; it was the library. There were so many books and gold and silver decorative objects. As good investigators, they looked left and right intently. There was so much money invested in that room. Phew!

"Good afternoon, gentlemen! Please, take a seat," said a good-looking man who promptly entered the library through a door on the other side of the room. It was Egurmendi himself.

They greeted each other and sat down.

"We learned . . ." said Garaidi gingerly, "that you just lost your father, and we would like to express our condolences. These are not easy days, and that's why, without taking too much of your time, we would like to wrap up our conversation."

Egurmendi offered them a cigarette.

"We," began Garaidi once more, "work on cases that people hire us to investigate. And we are working on a small case here, in Urgain."

Egurmendi looked impassive. Not even a grimace. Nothing.

"It's about an old event," said Patxi, without lifting his eyes from Egurmendi. "But we thought that you could clarify something for us . . ."

"Glad to be of help. Continue, continue!"

"Someone has asked us to track down or find out what happened to a certain Pagodi fellow who went missing in Urgain some years ago," Patxi told him straightforwardly, without beating about the bush, and kept his eyes fixed on him, trying to guess what Egurmendi was thinking.

"That is surely not a new story," replied Egurmendi calmly.

"You're right, it's been years since it happened, but they've hired us for this job and we must do our best . . ."

"Others did their best then, too. I don't think you'll be able to find out anything new. I'm afraid you'll just waste your time . . ."

"He was your friend, wasn't he?" interjected Patxi.

"Yes, a very good friend! We got along very well; we were always together. Yes, I haven't forgotten . . ."

He remained quiet for a short while. The other two were all ears; no choked words, not even a clearing of his throat. They were all eyes, too; even the smoke coming from his cigarette didn't quiver. Was that composure real? Who knew! His face, at least, did not reflect any trace of worry that he might've been feeling inside.

"I haven't forgotten him. Pagodi was a good friend. He was my dearest friend of all. No, I haven't forgotten him," he explained calmly.

He held a beautiful wooden ashtray and said:

"Look at this, he made it with his own hands. He gave it to me many years ago and I always keep it with me."

It was beautiful, a representation of two men and a woman holding hands, extraordinary work.

Garaidi took it and read what Pagodi had written by hand underneath: "To Joxe, from the bottom of my heart, (signed) the craftsman." One side of the ashtray had cracked and a splinter had almost broken off.

I am not sure what sort of urge overcame Garaidi right then to break off that splinter. A ridiculous suspicion darted through his mind like a lightning flash. He had a hunch that it would help the case.

Impulse and action! A small crunch and, without anyone noticing, he hid the splinter in his pocket.

"What do you think happened to Pagodi?" asked Patxi in the meantime.

"What can I say, I don't know."

"Didn't your wife pass away that same day?"

"Yes, the very same day . . ."

"She was young, wasn't she? What happened?"

"Typhus . . ."

"Contagious, then."

"Yes, we had to bury her quickly."

"Where you with her when she died?" he asked, prodding him.

"Yes."

He didn't show even a hint of anxiety. He was oblivious to what happened, perhaps. They were amazed, seeing Egurmendi's restraint.

They lingered for a time, chatting there, hoping to obtain more information about Pagodi, but from Egurmendi's lips, they found out very little.

Egurmendi explained that the day his wife died hadn't been the best day to worry about the dealings of others, but they were sure that Pagodi didn't make it to their house that day. He could not suspect his servants. It was preposterous to think of it. At that time, they had a total of four servants and maids. Two of them had since passed away, because they were old even back then. Both were straighter than arrows. Another one was still a maid at his service; she was a little slow-witted. The fourth — Pirmin, the servant we know — was visiting his hometown. No! They wouldn't be able to find out anything following the servants.

"Was your wife a foreigner?" asked Garaidi, beginning to feel bored because he wasn't getting anywhere.

"Yes, she was from Belgium. We got married there. That's her." And he showed them a photo displayed on a shelf.

An attractive woman was the only impression Patxi had, but Garaidi's heart skipped a beat when he saw the photograph. She looked identical to Begoña. They looked like twins or . . . my God . . . like mother and daughter!

Garaidi's head was ready to explode, what confusion! What the devil was all this?

Was Begoña Egurmendi's daughter, then? But . . . that was crazy. He had heard that Egurmendi's wife had died before Begoña was born. That was a trick! Were they sisters, perhaps? Or . . . was Begoña older than she said, and had she been born before the Egurmendis married?

They did their best, probing him here and there, keeping their ears open but their mouths shut. They did not say anything about Muñube's escape; nothing about Pirmin and Muñube's fight; nothing about the pin; they did not mention what they learned in Begoña's house, let alone what they saw in the grave.

They left Egurmendi's house saying that they would return if they had any other questions. Garaidi's head was spinning wildly. Sisters? . . . Mother and daughter?. . . What a mystery!

20

# Larrola's Confession

Sunday afternoon is usually a time for rest, but there were some, in addition to Garaidi, immersed in hard, inner-work. One of them was doctor Larrola whom they found sheltered by the doorway of Joxe Jokin's inn, shrunken by fright, perhaps by the sound of their approaching footsteps.

"I was waiting for you."

What a sight. He looked pitiful!

"Let's go in."

It was too early for dinner, so the dining room was empty. They sat at a table right there, in a corner. They listened attentively to what Larrola had to say. He went around and around like a lost ant.

"He is here to confess something," thought Garaidi.

"I'm here to confess something," he mumbled.

"Tell us," Garaidi encouraged him softly, while thinking: "He's done something."

"I've done something," he started.

He started and stopped.

"I . . . well . . . yesterday . . . I mean . . . well . . . I . . ."

He hesitated, but finally exploded:

"Has Muñube shown up?" he asked, eagerly.

"No."

"Then . . ."

"He told Muñube about what we saw in the grave," thought Garaidi.

"Then . . . It's my fault . . . I told him about . . . what we saw in the grave."

Haltingly, he related the conversation he had with Muñube. Now, all shriveled up, he didn't look anything like the slender Larrola they first met.

"You must believe me; I told him about what we saw, thinking that he already knew," he said, overcome by embarrassment. "Later, I realized that he didn't know anything at all, but it was too late. I had already spilled it! I've had the worst day! The hours came and went and I wanted to tell you about it, but I couldn't bring myself to. I looked for Muñube but I couldn't find him. You sure made me sweat when you stopped by my house this morning. I almost told you what happened but I couldn't. I was a basket case. I couldn't stand it any longer and I came to confess."

Garaidi was furious. He didn't keep his word. He let him down. What an unreliable man!

However, he didn't show him his anger. After all, he had come to confess. Besides, didn't this confession shed some light on Muñube's escape? Now he was certain that they were talking about an escape. Yes, they had to find Muñube. This should be their priority, to find Muñube!

They unsuccessfully searched long and hard, all over Urgain. He didn't return to the inn or to Amunda's house, either. The upstairs, tangle-haired neighbor didn't know anything; she must not have been a witch, after all. In Txomin's house, a nest of worries for two, they did not know anything; Egurmendi hadn't left his house; at about eleven, Begoña called from Donostia, wondering if Muñube was home; they had to figure out a new lie. Joxe Jokin, on the other hand, kept sleeping in his room with the door locked from the inside.

Finally, frustrated and restless, turning their thoughts to dinner, they made for Donostia. They were starving!

But, before that, they went to see a friend who was a chemist and left him the small splinter he stole at Egurmendi's house. All three knew what had to be done.

21

# Monday: Muñube Returns!

For the last hour they hadn't taken their eyes off that house. It was twelve-thirty. They were starting to get bored. It had been a very long hour. It must've been about eleven when that urchin handed him his man's note.

"It's been awhile now, Justino. It's beginning to worry me . . ."

They were crammed inside Garaidi's small car. After all, don't Americans say that one can't "drive" a European car, that you instead "wear" it?

And there they were, hanging on, spying. It wasn't an easy task.

Earlier that Monday morning, at about ten o'clock, Egurmendi had taken his car and had left home. Justino, Garaidi's reliable assistant, before Egurmendi had driven too far, quickly got in his car, too, and was right behind. He followed Egurmendi closely, driving all the way to Donostia. Once there, without straying, Egurmendi stopped in front of an apartment building at 45 Legazpia Street. And, it goes without saying, Justino stopped right behind him. By then he was on top of things and quickly realized who lived there. It was Muñube's parents' place. Well, well, why is Egurmendi coming to their home? he wondered. Wolves don't hurt their own kind. But who's the real wolf here? This doesn't look good.

He had a hunch that there was something suspicious there and he got a street kid to bring his boss a message: "I am on 45 Legazpia Street, tracking Egurmendi. Hurry over here." And that's where they were.

Egurmendi's behavior was suspicious. Why did he go to Muñube's house? It was true that the Egurmendi family had a very close relationship with Muñube's brother, Urgain's doctor? But now, after all that happened, why did Egurmendi come to Muñube's brother's house?

They waited . . . Twelve-thirty; twelve forty-five; one o'clock . . . and:

"Shh!" said Garaidi. "Look who's coming!"

He was right. Young Muñube was walking on the other side of the street. Hadn't they looked for him everywhere for the last two days? There he was, cool-as-can-be, headed straight to his parents' house, as if nothing had happened. What kind of malicious plan had he concocted now? Had he lured Egurmendi with lies? Or were they accomplices?

He couldn't waste any time considering different scenarios and afraid of what they were plotting, Garaidi made a decision on the spot.

"Justino, I'm going to confront him. You watch Egurmendi."

He got out of the car at once and, as if it were pure coincidence, encountered Muñube, who seemed surprised, staring at Garaidi in awe. Surprised, but not distressed.

"Good morning, Muñube. I've been looking for you since yesterday."

"Well, here I am."

"Where have you been all this time?"

"What do you care?" he retorted.

"Me? I'm not sure, but I think there's something we should discuss. Where have you been?"

"Visiting a cousin who is sick. So what?"

"Really? Does he live far away?

"In Gasteiz. I left Saturday evening."

"Alone?"

"Yes."

"And you decided to leave on the spur of the moment?"

"Yes. So what?"

"You didn't even have time to let Joxe Jokin know you wouldn't be there for dinner?"

"Has that old tattletale babbled again? I just forgot to let him know."

"And your girlfriend, too?"

"Why don't you leave my girlfriend out of this? Get lost! Are you spying on me?" he asked hotly.

"What are you talking about? Me, spying on you? Didn't you hire me for a job?"

"What does that have to do with my girlfriend?"

"Do you know where the Amundas are?" he asked, taking another angle.

"Me? I couldn't care less where they are. Why should I?"

"It looks like you don't know anything. Have you also forgotten what Larrola told you last Saturday?" he asked him sharply.

Muñube looked him straight in the eyes.

"Yes, Muñube. Larrola told me everything. Why are you trying to hide things? For everyone's sake, why don't you tell me openly everything you know? Eh? Why not? Should I infer from your unwillingness to speak that you're involved in some wrongdoing? Should I figure that you're on the run? There's something twisted here, Muñube, very twisted. C'mon, put that attitude aside and tell me the truth."

"You think I'm lying . . ."

"Lying? Is it true that your uncle gave you the lapel pin?"

And astonishingly for Garaidi, instead of going berserk and yelling in an uproar, as Garaidi might have expected, Muñube bowed his head, buried his chin in his chest and turned redder than a child with chickenpox.

By then, Justino had gotten out of the car in case Garaidi needed him. He was lingering by Muñube discreetly, without losing sight of the house, in case Egurmendi came out. There was no sign of him yet. What could he be doing up there?

"Where are you headed?" asked Garaidi.

"I was going to my parents to have lunch."

Was he telling the truth? Garaidi wasn't sure. Was he going to have lunch or look for Egurmendi?

"Let's get in my car for a minute. I'd like to ask you a few questions."

That was the perfect time to find out a few things from Muñube.

Iron, as the saying goes, has to be forged while it's hot.

22

# Muñube's Confession

"I didn't know anything until the day before yesterday, when Larrola told me about it," said an annoyed Muñube in fits and starts. "I didn't know anything about the graveyard discovery. How would I know? Do you remember how you once told me that I held a grudge against Egurmendi? I loved Karmentxo; true. And I hoped to marry her; true. But in those days, I was a lazy bum with no job and, truth be told, I wasn't a very desirable suitor for her. Most likely, that's why she did not consider me, and it was over. But . . . from that, to say that because she began seeing Egurmendi, I hate him . . . What do I care about Karmentxo when I love Begoña now? But, it might be true that, deep inside, I have some hate for Egurmendi. He is a year older than me and I've known him since childhood. Though his father and my uncle were very close friends, we were never close. We had no fondness for each other. Apparently, I was not worthy of his friendship. I was not a suitable friend for that big shot. He figured I had nothing to offer him. Such a pompous ass!"

What was this, bitterness or envy?

"Nevertheless," he continued as before; grudgingly, with eyes downcast, "at least for these last years I haven't been bothered by it. But after hearing my uncle's deathbed nightmares, I began paying attention to his life. And then, that letter . . ."

"What letter?"

"The letter I found among my uncle's things right after his death. It had been written about the time Pagodi disappeared, by the recently departed Egurmendi Sr. With great tenderness, he told my uncle this, more or less: that he knew he was in debt to him; that in God's name, keep quiet about what happened to Pagodi; not to tell anyone about that death."

"You don't have the letter here by any chance?"

"No, I don't. But that's why I began to suspect Egurmendi. Could it be true, what my uncle said on his deathbed?"

"And, where were you at that time" interrupted Garaidi, urging him.

"I was . . . in Madrid. Why?" he replied, as if to say: "I don't know anything, nothing, I don't know anything."

"No reason. And . . . you're not afraid that you might tarnish your uncle's good name by involving him in this mess?"

"Tarnish my uncle's good name? No, I'm not afraid of that. Not at all. If only everyone were like my uncle! The Egurmendis, not my uncle, they, they are the ones I thought were suspicious. I was very confused, of course. Everyone held them in such high esteem, but what were they truly like? Were they as decent as they seemed in the eyes of the people in Urgain, or were they nothing but vile and greedy? I had my doubts. But, when Larrola told me about the gravesite, my doubts were over. His wife killed by a bullet, and they kept it a secret? What does that mean? What else! Only one thing! That they did her in! First, the woman, and later, why not Pagodi, too? Wouldn't they have reported it if it had been someone else? Wouldn't they have spread it to the four winds? Wouldn't they have turned the village inside out looking for the killer? Needless to say, they would have. Then, who's the killer, if not them? My uncle was right. He sure was! He knew something. These criminals! A famous name, but a rotten one!"

"If what you say is right, your uncle's actions don't look very good. It looks like he was part of a cover-up," interrupted Garaidi, once more.

"I don't think so . . . "

They were still inside his car, sitting next to each other. Muñube first felt enraged and later annoyed; assertive for a moment and insecure the next; agitated, yet listless; sharp, but apathetic; agile, yet awkward . . . Garaidi hung on to each word. Muñube didn't see anything beyond his own nose; Garaidi, on the other hand, tried to penetrate Muñube's mind, whose heart boiled, ready to overflow; Garaidi, kept his head. There was still no trace of Egurmendi.

"Taking all this into consideration," Muñube said, gushing in scattered bursts, "how could I allow Karmentxo to be with him? No way! As soon as I heard the horrible news from Larrola, I left him in my room and, without realizing that I hadn't even had supper yet, rushed to Karmentxo's house . . . Convinced that something needed to be done immediately, I told her father everything in detail, without any nonsense. You can only imagine his fear and anxiety. How could we let Karmentxo spend another day alone with Egurmendi? While we talked in one room, mother and daughter remained in the kitchen, surprised to see me, of course. At that late hour, who would show up but me? From my former relationship with Karmentxo, they could tell I was worked up. They were speechless. In the end, we decided to leave Urgain as soon as possible. We were afraid Egurmendi might've known you had discovered the skull. If Egurmendi were to find out that the news of the crime had spread, we were afraid he could come looking for Karmentxo. We were so fearful. Who knew what a crazy person like that could do? Amunda, too, of course, was terrified. There was a train bound for Madrid at one in the morning, and we decided to catch it to go to Gasteiz. But we had to come up with a lie to convince mother and daughter to make such an unexpected trip. How, how could we tell them the truth? Should we tell them this, should we tell them that . . . ? Finally, we told them that I heard there was going to be a huge workers' strike in Urgain; that they expected the use of force and even shootings and that we should leave while we could. They panicked! They were beside themselves. And then we did it as planned. We left for Gasteiz."

Garaidi willingly listened to Muñube's story. Was he telling the truth? Was he lying? Who knew!

"Where did Begoña's parents obtain the lapel pin?" Garaidi asked with eager interest.

"Well . . . I'm not sure. When she gave it to me she said it had belonged to her father. I don't believe she lied. If I had known it belonged to Pagodi! What were the chances of you realizing it was Pagodi's as soon as you saw it? Yes, I must admit that I lied to you when I said the pin belonged to my uncle, but I lied only to keep from involving Begoña in this mess. That's all. I wasn't trying to hide anything. I don't believe Begoña knew it had belonged to Pagodi. No way!"

"Have you known Begoña for a long time?"

"Not really. Six months. But don't try scaring me. She's innocent! Poor thing."

He kept talking about Begoña, Begoña this, Begoña that for quite a while, trying to make his girlfriend look good.

Today, at least, Garaidi thought that Muñube was telling the truth but, still . . . Garaidi kept wishing that he knew as much as Joxe Jokin. The old man was so sure that Muñube was guilty. And here was Muñube so convinced that Egurmendi was the guilty one. One of the two had to be wrong . . . wrong, or consumed in a lie. Who knew!

Muñube, by then, had calmed down and persisted trying to absolve himself and Begoña from any wrongdoing. Was he innocent after all, or was he nothing but an excellent actor? Wanting to know this answer and wondering if he might burst, what should happen but, bang, Garaidi saw Egurmendi come out of the house and leaving his car where it had being parked all that time, entered an inn across the street. He asked Muñube abruptly:

"Why did you make Egurmendi come to your parents' house?"

"What?" he said, taken aback.

Yes, no question, if he were not innocent, Muñube was an amazing actor. He looked as if he had just awakened.

"Look, there's his car."

"That one? . . . Sure! . . . And he's at my parents' house?" he asked completely confused and restless.

"Yes. You didn't know?"

"Me? . . . He's liable to kill my parents. That bastard! If anything has happened . . ."

He was so angry that he threw off sparks. He was beside himself with rage, his hatred palpable, ready to explode.

Suddenly, in mid-conversation, he lit off in a whirl toward his parents' house.

What was Egurmendi doing in their house? Were his parents all right? Would he arrive in time? Why didn't Garaidi say something sooner? Jackass! To conceal such information! Had he lost his mind?

In an instant, he was at the house ringing the doorbell while Garaidi followed him with a smirk on his face.

"If I catch him . . ." Muñube said clenching his fists in wild fury. "He's going to get what his servant didn't. I'm going to crush his skull!"

He was beside himself with indignation.

Riiiiiiiiiing!! . . . Riiiiiiing! . . .

And . . .

23

# Sparks Fly. . .

Muñube Sr. was as broad-shouldered as his son but taller, a lot taller! From head to toe, he must've been seven feet. Bones and all, he must've weighed at least two hundred and thirty pounds. Under his nose, he had two bushes of white hair sticking straight out. On his forehead he displayed a small, purplish birthmark that resembled a bird dropping. His overall impression was that of a scoundrel. And he was! His hair had now turned to grey, but in his youth, when his hair was coal black, next to the mark on his forehead, he had a single shock of white hair. He was so tall that the white forelock resembled a perpetually snow-covered mountain-peak. That was the reason, in his childhood, his friends nicknamed him 'Mulazen.'

Because of self-consciousness or rejection caused by that birthmark, perhaps, even from a young age, he had been a mean and selfish person. He did not warm up to others easily. As years came and went, the color of his hair had softened, turning white, but his character did not. And that particular day, apparently, had not been one of his nicest.

As soon as his son said, "*aita,*" without asking who Garaidi was or why they had come, enraged, and, as if on fire, he brusquely interrupted:

"Where have you been?" he scolded him.

With arms as long as oars, stretching upward as if he had won a rowing competition:

"You are going to make me go crazy!" he said, incensed. "Everyone is looking for you and . . . you? Where were you? Lazy bum! Must we always be looking for you? Your girlfriend, later a short-legged guy, Joxe Jokin, one of your lazy friends named Garaidi or something, that new doctor in Urgain, and finally, just now, Egurmendi . . . all looking for you and . . . you? Where were you?"

Yes. They caught him at a bad time. A rough time, indeed!

Garaidi, trying to calm him down, agreed with him, but for a stubborn brute like that there's nothing worse than siding with him, and the result was disastrous. It was like adding straw to a fire, like pouring rain on puddles.

It was amazing how he acted . . . and yet more amazing what they found out through him.

No, Egurmendi hadn't come planning to kill him. He didn't come with evil intentions.

"Egurmendi . . ." he said, "after he realized

you were nowhere to be found in Urgain, came looking for you. This is what he wanted to give you. Here!" He threw a bunch of money on the table. "He brought it for you! It's for you . . ."

That was serious money!

"Forty-thousand pesetas! Yours!"

Later, after he calmed down a little, he explained how it all happened. Apparently, the late Egurmendi had left that money for the young Muñube. This is what Egurmendi Jr. said, word-for-word, repeating what Egurmendi's last will stated: "As a small token of appreciation for all invaluable favors that his uncle did for me, I would like to have forty-thousand pesetas go to Felipe's nephew so that he may complete his medical school studies, so he may become as good a doctor as his uncle." That's all.

That's all . . . that's a lot! Not a mere token gift!

As the sea crashes against the rocks, creating splashing, foamy whirlpools during high tide, so did all the amazing information Muñube learned during the last days compete to overtake his mind. Without a word, he stood staring at the money, while biting on one of his fingers, and stood with a blank expression.

"So? What do you say?" asked his father, infuriated.

But what could he say? That he was overjoyed? That with that money he could finish his studies, become a doctor, buy a house, get married soon, live happily and . . . and . . . on and on? When he really was not thinking any of those things?

"What's wrong with you?"

There was nothing wrong with him, not at all. He could see everything with more clarity than ever before!

He began to regret having shared information with Garaidi, who was standing by quietly, all ears. How was he going to be able to tell him again, like he did earlier, that he was not afraid of impugning his uncle's good name next to Egurmendi's? Many ugly thoughts came to mind. But . . . what "favors" did his uncle perform to help Egurmendi? Was he referring to the gravesite? To Pagodi's disappearance, perhaps? What was it?

"Inaxio!" said his father, angry, once again. "Are you going to act like an idiot? Aren't you going to say anything? You should thank him . . . thank him, indeed!"

It didn't seem that the father knew anything. Was he asking him to thank Egurmendi? Nothing could be further from his son's mind.

# 24

# Herriburu Worries

Days had come and gone and, truth be told, in the past week Garaidi had hardly solved anything. Wasn't he such a clever man? It was embarrassing. And in Herriburu's opinion, the little he had found out, had made things worse.

Later that afternoon, when all this was on his mind, Herriburu said to Garaidi when he came to the house, "Joxe Jokin is convinced that Muñube is guilty; on the other hand, Muñube, in an effort to clear himself, accuses Egurmendi; Egurmendi says he doesn't know anything. You have definitely tightened this knot. What a huge mess. I'm afraid, Martin . . ."

"Afraid?"

"Yes, Martin, we can expect anything from Muñube's evil heart. Even daring to accuse Egurmendi of wrongdoing! That's incredible! When are you going to lock him up so we all can rest finally?"

Garaidi looked at him in bewilderment.

"Lock up Muñube? Why?"

"Well, didn't Joxe Jokin tell you that, without a doubt, Muñube is guilty?"

"C'mon now," interrupted Garaidi grinning, "Joxe Jokin says so many things . . . words are cheaper by the pound. Among all that talk, you have to throw some out. No, my friend, no. Joxe Jokin didn't know anything with certainty, as you seem to think. I was able to debunk his feeble theories in no time. The father of his knowledge was ignorance, and its mother . . . nothing but imagination. Imagination. That is often the source of such knowledge. Do you know the basis of his theory about that lapel pin? I'm not sure how, but it looks like Joxe Jokin got a hold of the newspapers that I brought to Muñube. He's a sharp, old man and he deduced that the pin in the newspaper and Muñube's were the same one. Pagodi disappeared and Muñube was in possession of Pagodi's pin? What else did he need? It was clear for the old man. Muñube killed Pagodi . . . that was all. It was easy. If it's not cold, it's hot . . . if it's not white, it's black.

"It's not that bad of a conclusion."

"Bad? Not bad . . . very bad! Worse than bad! Do you think that our knots are unraveled that easily? No, my friend, no. You know that Muñube's girlfriend gave him the pin."

"If that were true! Do not believe it, Martin!

So says that liar, but . . ."

"No. It wasn't him," Garaidi interrupted him, a bit harshly. "The one who first told me about it was the woman at Begoña's house. Don't forget it! And I doubt that she was trying to put the blame on Egurmendi's shoulders, too."

They were quiet for a while. Garaidi had come to Herriburu's house to inform him about his up-coming trip abroad, to keep him updated on the latest developments, and to say goodbye. And why not tell it like it was? Garaidi also wanted to talk to someone who would speak in favor of Egurmendi. Was it so hard to believe in his innocence? Did he see Egurmendi's name in such a dark light? There wasn't anyone better than Herriburu to speak fondly about Egurmendi. But by now, his strong conviction had begun to waver.

"Muñube, that lazy bum, innocent . . ." he said, talking to himself and looking nowhere in particular. "Muñube innocent and Egurmendi guilty . . . ?"

He looked Garaidi right in the eye and said:

"Is Egurmendi guilty?" he began. "Did you come here to tell me that? C'mon now, don't be on the fence."

Garaidi remained quiet.

"Such an upstanding man . . ." he began once more, using a rather angry tone, shifting his gaze from one side of the floor to the other. "He is so proper in appearance . . .and now this?"

“True,” agreed Garaidi as if he were sad. “Egurmendi’s name is not clear yet. What I found about him doesn’t make him look good.”

“To kill his own wife? . . . My Lord!!” said Herriburu.

He held his head between his hands and sat, looking resigned, on the edge of a chair.

“And Pagodi, too,” he said under his breath.

“I’m not worried about that,” said Garaidi, trying to confuse Herriburu.

Herriburu looked at him raptly. What was Garaidi up to now?

“I’m not worried about that,” he repeated. “It’s been twenty years since Pagodi disappeared, but Pagodi, as far as I know, was alive eight years ago.”

“Alive?” asked Herriburu completely taken aback. ”Where did you come up with that information?”

“Where? Well, when I went to Egurmendi’s house, I stole a small splinter and . . . that was it.”

Herriburu sat more comfortably and listened closely.

What Garaidi had to say was truly interesting . . .

“Listen . . .”

## 25

# Is It Witchcraft?

"From beyond the sun, all the way from the stars," Garaidi began again, slowly, "invisible, weak rays of light are constantly being projected at us. When those rays enter our atmosphere, they create drops of lightning. Those blasts collide with the nitrogen in our air and turn into a special kind of carbon. One of the peculiarities of this carbon is its ability to transform. This unique carbon gradually and continuously dissipates while emitting radiation. Through this process, as it dissipates and regenerates, it becomes a great percentage of our earth's air, which we breathe. That being said, observe what happens next.

"Plants also absorb or 'eat' this carbon dioxide gas and, consequently, it becomes a component of the structure of the plant. Animals and insects that consume these plants convert this carbon into an important part of their structure as well. Then, what happens when those plants, insects and animals perish? Here's what: this unique carbon gradually disintegrates and, because it doesn't regenerate as air, finally, it disappears!

"All this is rigorously measured. An American, Mr. Libby, the inventor of the Radiocarbon Dating Method, stated that it takes 5,568 years for half the carbon in an original sample to decay and, after another 5,568 years, half of that remaining carbon will have decayed, and so on.

"Thus, we always know the amount of carbon in the air; we know the percentage of this unique carbon in the body of each living plant, insect and animal; we also know how much of it disappears in the air if it doesn't get regenerated by being absorbed or 'eaten'. On the other hand, we can measure the remaining percentage of this type of carbon out of other components in wood, bones and flesh; in anything that has had life at some point. And, of course, once we know that, it is very easy to find out when the tree from which that wood came, or the animal to whom those bones belonged, stopped absorbing that carbon, when they stopped eating; in other words, to find out when they died. These are complex measurements, true, but they can be made."

Herriburu was openmouthed listening to all this. He was clearly impressed with Garaidi's explanations. Garaidi was on fire, confident and persuasive.

"And this is exactly," he continued, "what I

did. I've had a chemist analyze the levels of that unique carbon in the splinter I took from the wooden ashtray that Pagodi made by hand. This measurement will tell us when the tree from which that splinter came, was cut."

He extracted a card from his pocket and said:

"Here are the conclusions," 'seven years, eight at most.' So . . . What do you say?"

For Herriburu all this was like witchcraft. But you had to believe it. This is the type of thing devoted to the scholar.

"So, that means that Pagodi carved the ashtray sometime during the last eight years," he digressed, grinning.

He was delighted! Ecstatic! Truly, wasn't it enough of a reason to be overjoyed, knowing, without a doubt, that Egurmendi hadn't killed Pagodi? Now, in regards to the other matter Garaidi was investigating, how could he believe that Egurmendi had killed that woman? Preposterous!

Once again, Herriburu began pacing the room, but this time he didn't look as pale as he did earlier; instead, he felt like taking action and doing something immediately.

"And? What's next?" he asked impatiently.

After Garaidi stubbed his cigarette repeatedly to extinguish it, he replied calmly:

"From the very beginning, Pirmin looked suspicious to me. Of course! You know where I met him. That encounter was enough to give me a bad feeling. Pirmin knows something."

He looked down at the floor and didn't say a word for a moment, as he seemed to want to organize his thoughts.

"Do you know were I was yesterday and the day before? " he asked him suddenly.

Herriburu did not answer him but one could see the wonder all over his face.

"In Pirmin's hometown, and . . . I'm having trouble," he continued, "wrapping my head around some information I learned there. But I don't think I'm too far from solving this mystery. I'm not there yet, though."

Herriburu stood facing Garaidi, completely quiet, his legs in a wide stance with his hands in his pockets and eyes fixed on him.

"At the time Pagodi disappeared," resumed Garaidi, "I read all the interviews that were given, one by one, and . . . do you know something? Pirmin was never mentioned. It's just noted that he was not there and that he was in his hometown on his days off, that's all. At that time, they didn't seem to think this was important but I say: If Pirmin was the most-trusted servant, if he was like a part of the family and was so loved, how come he wasn't at home after the lady of the house passed away? It was understandable . . . if he wasn't there that day . . . because she passed unexpectedly. But why didn't he come at once as soon as he learned the news? How could that be? That is why I was dumbfounded. Why didn't he come back? You tell me! Why not?"

Herriburu was speechless, not knowing how to answer.

"I haven't learned much in his hometown," Garaidi said, more evenly now, "but the little I have learned is quite meaty. Pirmin wasn't in his hometown during those days."

"He wasn't?'

"No. They lied about it here. I found out something else, too, but I don't see how it fits with this case. Yet, somehow, it must. Yes, it must! Did you know Pirmin's sister?"

"I didn't even know he had a sister. And . . . ?" he prompted, seeing that Garaidi had grown quiet. "What's your next move?"

"I'm going to France tomorrow, to Begoña's hometown. At that time no one 'sniffed around' there, and I am hopeful that I might find the stray-end of our knot there."

"I hope you do!"

26

# Thursday: Egurmendi and Pirmin

The noon Bilbao-Donostia train passed by Eibar and was nearing the coast. A stout, scowling man that we've already met had boarded in Bilbao. It was Pirmin. As they rode along in a soft mist, none of the villages, mountains, farmhouses, fields, forests and creeks caught his attention. The beauty of the surroundings did not bring him any tranquility, did not cheer him. Was he angry? No, it wasn't anger, but anxiety. That was it. He received a suspicious communication and he was worried sick.

He kept thinking: "Who's this Garaidi? What does he want from me? If I only knew!"

When they passed Deba, something, the smell of the sea perhaps, pulled him out of himself and, after getting more comfortable in his seat, he took a wrinkled telegram from his pocket, raised it to his eyes and began reading it for the tenth time:

"For your own good and the chance to get the

latest about Pagodi, I'll be waiting for you at 35 Loiola Street, next Thursday, at four o'clock. Garaidi."

No, he wasn't dreaming. He was holding that wrinkled, disturbing piece of paper right before his eyes. Definitely not a dream.

He rubbed his eyes and remained half-reclined in his seat, looking straight ahead. Straight into his own thoughts.

"What has this Garaidi found out about Pagodi? Who is he?" he kept wondering.

A number of years had passed since Pagodi 'disappeared' and, gradually, Pirmin's constant internal pang of fear had dissipated. It would have to be now, after he had left Urgain behind, now that he lived in Bilbao, gotten married, was surrounded by his wife's love and their children's joy, now that he had a job, a new life, a new routine and new relationships that had nearly made him forget the dark days he spent in Urgain. It would have to be now! Now, when he felt protected behind a curtain of thick fog of the passing years, now when he lived more peacefully than ever. Damn it!

Two weeks earlier, at the Urgain inn, his heart had skipped a beat when he saw that man openly and brazenly showing Pagodi's lapel pin. And he sure sweated bullets trying to get out of that fight in one piece. He did not want to imagine if they had taken him for a thief . . . if they thought he was trying to steal that pin. Better not to think about it.

And now, when the black eyes from the fight still hadn't healed, now, two weeks later, he received this communication. Was this a direct consequence of that fight? Was this Garaidi character the man he fought? What a strange and suspicious message.

When he first read the telegram, he thought: "Go to Donostia to talk about Pagodi? Me? Are you kidding? I'm not going. There's no way. No way."

But what could he do? Run away to America? Hide in a cave? Just ignore it? What a quandary!

He did not tell his wife anything about the message. What for? It would only frighten her. Finally, after spending two long days carefully considering and calculating the pros and the cons of that message, he told his wife he had to take care of some business in Donostia. Now he was headed there, come what may.

More than once he had contemplated calling or writing to Egurmendi but, after what happened, how was he going to risk having his call intercepted? What if someone uncovered everything? Was he doing the right thing? Was he mistaken?

It was too late to do anything about it now. It might be better to decide what to do by himself, anyway. Besides, who said this Garaidi had contacted him with bad intentions? Hadn't he said, 'For your own good?' Was he looking for blackmail to keep something quiet? If that were it, he would shut him up at once! What could he have learned after so many years, anyway? He couldn't know much. And what little Garaidi may know, he could always deny. That's that!

Two hours later, as he rang Garaidi's doorbell, he was frightened once again. What awaited him behind the door?

" I am Pirmin Elurzabal from Bilbao. Is the man of the house at home?" he nervously announced to the maid who opened the door. What if she said he wasn't there? He would be so relieved!

"Come in . . . just a minute."

His wishes did not come true.

She opened the door to a room and invited him to enter.

Someone else was in that room, apparently also waiting for Garaidi. The fact that someone else was there too was not so surprising, but the person waiting was none other than Egurmendi himself. What was this?

Both men looked at each other in awe. As soon as Pirmin entered the room and the maid closed the door and left:

"Why are you here?" both said in unison.

This was the type of room that lawyers, doctors and the like maintained as reception areas in their homes. There were quite a few chairs around the room and right in the middle there was a small table full of books and magazines. It wasn't extravagant but it was elegant and neatly kept.

As soon as Pirmin sat next to Egurmendi, they began to converse, interrupting each other, talking in half-whispers.

"Are you waiting for Garaidi?"

"Yes. And you?"

"I'm coming to see him, but . . ."

"Do you know him?"

"No, I don't. Do you?"

"Yes."

"Who is he?"

"A policeman."

"A policeman?"

"Something like that. He's a private investigator."

"How long have you known him?"

"He came to my house last week."

"Oh, yeah? How come?"

"He asked me about Pagodi. You haven't met him?"

"No. He asked me to come see him, and . . ."

"Me too."

"What do you think he wants?"

"To find out something about Pagodi. But I doubt he'll learn anything, from us anyway."

"Well, I'm nervous."

"I'm not."

"I sure made a narrow escape from Urgain."

"No kidding. How come you left without letting me know?"

"I got into a fight that night."

"A fight? What do you mean?"

"You wouldn't believe it. Do you remember that rare lapel pin that Pagodi owned? Some arrogant guy kept showing that pin to anybody that set foot at the inn."

"But what are you saying?" Egurmendi interrupted him, amazed. "Pagodi's pin? How did he get a hold of Pagodi's pin? Who was the guy?"

"How should I know? Someone who was staying at the inn."

"And who did you fight?"

"The same guy. When I saw him with the pin, I decided to snatch it from him, and went up to his room. But after turning the room upside down looking for it, I found it finally inside a small box and I took it. After putting everything back in its place, just as I was leaving the room . . . Bam! He caught me right there!"

"No way! And . . . ?"

"When I saw him standing at the door, in the dark, realizing that I could escape by hitting him in the face, I punched him, but he was no weakling and both of us fell to the floor, punching each other."

"You still have evidence around your eyes. And . . . ?"

"Nothing. Everyone heard the commotion and came up to see what was going on, and . . . I told them I went in the wrong room by mistake. A narrow escape! He, on the other hand, kept saying that he punched me, believing I was a thief. That jackass didn't even remember that I delivered the first punch."

"And the pin?"

"The pin? I must've dropped it during the fight, and the owner of the inn, that talkative old man, grabbed it and placed it in the box before anyone else saw anything."

"This doesn't look good," interrupted Egurmendi, downcast.

"I know. I agree. That's why I left and I didn't sleep there that night."

"There? I was there the next morning looking for you, oblivious to what had happened."

"Really? And what did they say?"

"Not much. Just that you were gone."

"I'm afraid this is the reason Garaidi called me."

"When I was with him before, he didn't mention anything about this."

"And what did you tell him when he asked you about Pagodi?"

"Me? Nothing. That I didn't know anything."

"If everything were to come out now, we would be doomed."

"I don't know. Let's hope it doesn't. Who

could have had Pagodi's pin? Could it be this Garaidi?"

"It was a short, husky guy, about forty years old."

"No, this one's not short."

"I don't know."

Both got quiet. One stared at the floor with his elbows on his knees, the other, on the edge of his chair drumming his fingers, gazed at a figurine in front of him. They had lots to think about.

"Lately everything is going wrong for me," said Egurmendi, his face showing all the darkness he kept bottled up inside.

"What else is going on?"

"Karmentxo has run away from me."

"Run away?"

"From one day to the next, without saying a word. And not only that, her parents are gone, too."

"Do you know where they have gone?"

"Yes, to Gasteiz, to her aunt's house."

"And, what does she have to say?"

"Say? Nothing."

"Haven't you called her?"

"You know me. Don't think that I'm full of myself but . . . she's the one who left . . . she's the one who should explain herself."

"Don't be so stubborn."

"Yes, Pirmin, yes. I love her dearly and I would even have accepted it, if she hadn't left with him

. . ."

"What?" Pirmin said as if asking, "what are you going to do?" because he thought it would be too harsh to ask 'with whom?'

"With Muñube," answered Egurmendi, guessing what Pirmin wanted to know.

"With Muñube? What Muñube?"

"The doctor's nephew."

"I remember that a little boy lived with him."

"That boy grew up, like us, Pirmin: he became a man. He had already chased her in the past so . . ."

"Seriously? I didn't know. Karmentxo is no fool, eh?"

"Apparently."

"You've had some fine days lately, haven't you? First your father died, then your fiancée ran away and now this new mess."

"New mess? The old turns new and the new gets old. By the way, wasn't Txomin surprised to see you at the cemetery?

"I don't think so, that sad sack."

"No one else saw you, eh?"

"I don't think so . . . I didn't run into anyone else."

Let's leave these two in their lively conversation and move on . . .

# 27

# Muñube, Larrola, and the Rest

Let's continue to another room in the same house. This also was a type of waiting room; a little less-elegant than the other but still well-appointed. In the room were two men who had arrived together an hour earlier. We've already met these gentlemen: Muñube Jr. and Dr. Larrola.

"He's obviously taking his time," said Muñube, beginning to tire of the waiting. "Didn't he tell us to be here at three o'clock sharp, for this? How inconsiderate!"

"Your escape has sure messed things up for the two of us," added Larrola, also put off by the long wait.

"Was it my escape or your loose tongue? Don't blame it all on me. You should've thought before opening your big mouth."

"The thought did come late, I'll admit. You, on the other hand, it seems, accomplished your escape with no thought at all . . . neither before nor after."

"Many times, even when one is not sure what to do, it's best to do something, at least."

"Sure, why not begin braying like a jackass! Now you have to face the music."

"True, but our actions are minor matters. I wouldn't like to be in Egurmendi's skin."

"Me neither. He's done. He won't be able to hold his head up. And . . . what do you think Garaidi is going to tell us today?"

"I wonder if he has solved the case. That'd be something. Isn't it obvious that Egurmendi was in the middle of it? Will he have some explanation?" said Muñube, accusingly. But then to himself: "and, what about my uncle?"

'When did Garaidi get back from France?"

"The day before yesterday, or so."

"I wonder what he wants from us."

"To play hide and seek . . ."

"Sure! To tickle your nostrils! I'm getting tired of waiting."

"Me, too."

Now let's go now to the dining room of the same house and listen. Here too, we find familiar faces: Garaidi and his wife, Mr. and Mrs. Herriburu, and Txomin.

Compared to the others, this group looks very calm. They have just had lunch and are waiting for those who have been summoned. Txomin, like a sparrow in a falcon's nest, looks timid among all the rich people. Garaidi looks thrilled. The others smile, but with fluttering hearts.

"So you've had a good trip," said Herriburu.

"Sure, if you think that going in a hundred directions is a good trip . . ."

"No, no. It's obvious that all your troubles have left you wilted," teased Maritxu.

"Go ahead and laugh. I'd like to see you in my shoes; go here, go there, freeze to death yesterday, roast today, soaking-wet tomorrow, bored here, frustrated there, out of breath now, exhausted later, sniffing here, sniffing there . . ."

"You sure have the right-sized nose for it," interjected his wife.

"Sure, laugh all you want. Didn't you say when I got back from my trip: 'Martin, sweetheart, . . .'" he continued, imitating his wife's voice, "'Darling, didn't you bring me something? Didn't you bring me back a beautiful dress from Paris?'"

"As if every time he goes somewhere he brings me something! An old, dirty piece of an *albarka* . . . advising me that it holds the fingerprints of the killer, that through it he'll identify him, not to touch it, not to dust it . . . This junk is taking over my house."

"Stop it," Maritxu cut in, roaring with laughter.

"You don't believe me?"

Herriburu looked at his watch and said, impatiently:

"Four-twenty. The first one arriving must be bored to death by now."

"Be quiet and wait," said Garaidi. "The last one will be here in no time."

"What if someone doesn't show up?"

"I doubt we have to worry. They won't be able to resist the bait I set out."

"Who's supposed to come?" asked Herriburu obstinately.

"You're sure dying to know, eh? Be quiet and listen. Be calm. I told you, easy does it."

"That's what you always say."

"Right. That's what being a man is all about. Dependability. Tell it like it is. Not like those who say, 'green' now, only to say 'red' later. Not like owls who go '*chub, chub*' in spring and '*meuka, meuka*' in fall," said Garaidi, half -laughing, noticing that Herriburu was dying to find out who was coming.

"Always say the same thing? Donkeys always say the same thing too: *heee-haw, heee-haw*!"

They all burst into laughter.

"Isn't it true, Txomin?" he asked him. "Does your donkey know how to say anything else?"

"Mine never went to school, so . . ." Txomin said, smiling and staying with the joke.

The doorbell rang for the third time.

"This is it! Here we have the last ones. Quiet now!" said Garaidi. And like he did before, walking on his tiptoes, quietly, he went to the front door and observed through the peephole.

When he confirmed they were the visitors he was expecting, he asked his maid:

"Bring them to my study and tell them that I'm on my way. Don't tell them anything else."

No one saw these last visitors: Karmentxo and her father.

"The're all here!" said Garaidi, returning to the dining room and before Herriburu could stick his nose outside. "Wait until I ask for you."

And he left, smiling, after giving them the evil eye.

# 28

# The General Assembly

The Amunda father and daughter did not look calm at all when Garaidi greeted and approached them.

"God bless and good afternoon! Please, sit down."

What did this stranger possibly want from them?

"We've never met, but I've heard about you more than once from my old friend Herriburu," he began, as the three of them sat down.

"We got your phone call and . . ." said Amunda.

"Of course. I'm about to tell you why I asked you to come . . ."

He lit a cigarette, which he offered Amunda, who declined. After a pause, he spoke to them softly:

"Inaxio, your nephew, hired me for a job, a small, investigative job. As I followed clues, I learned many things and, the deeper I got into my investigation, the more secrets I uncovered. I thought that you probably would like to know what I discovered and that's why I've asked you to come."

The elder Amunda could not have looked more worried as he stared at everyone in the room, waiting to hear what Garaidi had to say. He was the one who burned all the letters that Karmentxo and Egurmendi had exchanged and, to top that, he hadn't said a word to Karmentxo about the discovery at the cemetery. He had preferred to have his daughter think that Egurmendi fell out of love with her rather than discover he was a killer.

"You haven't met my wife, I know," said Garaidi, looking at Karmentxo, as if he had guessed what her father was thinking, "but you know Herriburu's wife, I bet. Both are in the dining room right now. Would you like to join them while we chat a bit?"

Those in the study and the dining room greeted each other, and Herriburu, Amunda, Txomin and Garaidi returned to Garaidi's study while the women stayed behind. Then, right after entering the room, Garaidi asked them to wait for a minute and left.

The three men in the room were all from Urgain. They had seen and talked to each other often, but now, not sure of what was going to happen, they didn't feel like talking and remained in complete silence.

They did not have to wait long. After a few minutes, Garaidi returned with Muñube and Larrola at his side.

"Here's that lazy bum!" thought Herriburu as soon as he saw Muñube. "What a conceited jerk! Once a snob, always a snob! He'll have to come down to earth today."

"That's the new doctor who we saw at the graveyard," thought Txomin. "I wonder why they asked me to come?"

"How come Inaxio didn't tell me he was coming here?" wondered Amunda.

"Sit down, sit down!" said Garaidi.

They all greeted each other with a head nod and sat. What were Garaidi's intentions?

"You'll need to wait a little bit more," said Garaidi, standing. "We're not all here, yet. When I bring the remaining guests, you'll be surprised, of course, but . . . until I finish what I have to tell you, try to relax."

He left the room once more and this time he returned with Egurmendi and Pirmin. None looked very happy to see them. Those entering the room were not just anybody off the street. What a storm was brewing! Indeed!

"He killed his wife and has the guts to show up here as if nothing happened! What's next?" thought Amunda. And what is this idiot from Donostia thinking? Does he know who we are? To have us all here like this. What a fool, yipping and yapping and carrying on."

But others were even angrier than Amunda. Muñube, for example, was furious, enraged, as if ready to pick another fight with Pirmin and having a hard time controlling himself. That night, at the inn, if he had known who he was and what his intentions were, he would've given him all he could handle and more. Thankfully, for their own good, Egurmendi and Pirmin were surrounded this time. Otherwise . . .

That evening, as they all gathered in his house, Garaidi was on edge, afraid that some angry character would go crazy and ruin his plan. He had reason enough to be worried. But nothing like that happened.

He was not afraid of Amunda, really. He carried quite a few years under his belt to begin throwing punches. Besides, he was a very humble man. No, no, he wouldn't make trouble. Egurmendi was well-bred and would likely keep his composure. Would Larrola, on the other hand, start poking here and there, trying to find answers? He ended up being nothing more than a blabbermouth. No, Larrola didn't worry him, either. He worried about Txomin even less. He was sure that Herriburu would be on his side at all times, unless Egurmendi set him off.

But, for now, there were two he had to keep an eye on (first things first), whom he should watch.

On one hand, Pirmin, seeing Muñube there, could get spooked and be capable of anything. On the other hand, if Muñube's temper were ignited, nothing could control his fists.

But, as I said, all of them, frowning and serious, just stared at each other sideways. They waited in complete silence for Garaidi to give his address.

It would have only taken a spark for that meeting to explode in flames. Gathered there were doves and sparrow hawks, lambs and wolves, pure and rotten, good and evil . . . Of course, each thought of himself blameless and his neighbor as evil. But truly, who there was the dove, the sparrow hawk, the lamb, the wolf; pure, rotten, good or evil? This one accused that one; that one blamed the other . . . everyone against the others. Each one thought he was in possession of the truth . . . yet most were wrong. It was quite an assembly, indeed.

29

# Garaidi, on the Right Track

"Gentlemen!" Garaidi began, carefully measuring his words. "I summoned you, one by one, without letting you know why. But, by now I'm sure that you have realized that what I'm about to tell you is of great importance. For, without knowing me very well, indeed, for some of you, without knowing me at all, you have accepted my invitation. And you're right. What I'm going to tell you is not an insignificant matter. All of you know a piece of what I am about to tell you. Some of you more than others, some of you might be right, others wrong, some of you might have known for a long time, others more recently, some of you might be angry about it, others not. I see you all scowling at me. Why not. I can imagine what you are thinking about me: 'Who does this man think he is to gather us all here? Who is he to talk to us in this manner? Why doesn't he tell me privately what he needs to tell me without summoning all of us?' I understand your uneasiness and that is why I ask you, please, be patient and listen to what I have to say."

For a short while he stared in silence at all assembled there and at that very moment he realized how quiet they had become. Instead of eight men it was as if there were no one in that room.

He cleared his throat.

"Two weeks ago," he began once again, "the mystery of someone called Pagodi, which you have heard before, resurfaced. Someone asked me to find out what happened to him." Muñube, seeing that his name hadn't been mentioned, relaxed a little bit. "I began working at once, and . . . to my surprise, before two days had gone by, I stumbled upon Pagodi's unique lapel pin. Who had it? One of you."

Someone shot a sharp sideways stare at Muñube and he, restless and worried, shifted in his seat.

"But, I wasn't the only one who recognized the pin," continued Garaidi. "It seems like one other person among you knew that the pin belonged to Pagodi and consequently there were some incidents . . ." Now Pirmin's ears were burning.

One man softly stroked his chin while another rubbed his eyes . . . As the saying goes, "a toothache draws the tongue toward the pain." Egurmendi and Pirmin felt safe as long as Garaidi kept taking about Pagodi and didn't mention anything about the secrets of the cemetery.

"But, that being said," Garaidi resumed, while everybody listened in complete silence, the pin was safely returned to its box. Since the pin belonged to Pagodi, I began tracing its origin. The person who had it when I began my investigation said that his uncle gave it to him." Muñube lowered his head a little "But this person lied. Actually, a woman who lived here in Donostia had given it to him. And following this thread, I learned something amazing in France. This woman, this young woman, is Pagodi's daughter!"

Egurmendi began biting his lip. Pirmin reacted, as if he had sat on an ant pile. Everyone else was dumbfounded, especially Muñube; Garaidi was referring to none other than his girlfriend. His heart pounded.

"Following the same path," Garaidi continued without hesitation, "this is what I uncovered about Pagodi: Contrary to what many believed, no one killed Pagodi. From now on the truth will be known, at least among us. Pagodi ran away! That's all! He ran away. Why? He must have had some reasons. Anyway, he ran to France, changed his name, got married and had a daughter, the one who had the pin in her possession. Where's Pagodi now? Well . . . he's dead. A train, in which he and his wife were traveling, derailed and plunged into a river. As fate woud have it, both of them died in the accident. It happened about five years ago. Their daughter was studying here and, after the accident, she continued her studies at the same school."

They all looked sideways at one another, especially at Egurmendi. He seemed calm as always, at least on the surface. Who knew what was going on inside!

"So, that's it; I solved what I was hired to investigate. Pagodi died about five years ago near Marseille, and his daughter lives here."

Egurmendi wondered who had hired Garaidi. "Sticking his nose in other's business. And . . . Pagodi's daughter was here, in Donostia? How could that be? We looked for her everywhere. Why didn't Pagodi let me know that he had sent her here? That damned pin!"

Garaidi paused for a moment, but no one said a word. They reckoned that this was not all he had to say, and they waited.

"But . . . as I kept pulling the thread," Garaidi continued, "I discovered some astounding things."

The looks on some of their faces said, "Go on, tell us more."

Pirmin felt a chill from head to toe; Egurmendi's neck veins bulged. What was he about to tell them now?

"The same day that Pagodi disappeared, a woman died in Urgain," said Garaidi.

Everyone froze as Pirmin, soaked in sweat,

suddenly stood up glancing at the door. Egurmendi shot him a piercing look, signaling him to sit back down.

"Sit down, sit down, gentlemen," Garaidi teased them. "The doors are under lock and key. Rest assured, no one can come in."

Pirmin remained still for an instant as if turned to stone, but quickly took a seat, gazing at Egurmendi in distress.

"As I said," Garaidi continued slowly, "that very same day, a woman died in Urgain. I've seen her corpse and, no one can deny that she died from a gunshot wound."

Pounding heartbeats could be heard in the silence. Even Herriburu suffered witnessing his friends' anguish. Garaidi told him repeatedly beforehand not to worry, but where was he headed? Even Egurmendi seemed worried now. Pirmin, seated next to him, looked as if the ant colony under his chair had multiplied. What a bloodletting!

"Who was this woman?" asked Garaidi, after a while. Why was he beating about the bush? Didn't they say that Egurmendi's wife had died that same day?

What could Egurmendi and Pirmin do after listening to that, but stay there until it was all over? Pirmin was sweating and Egurmendi looked grim. He thought: "When did he see that? Didn't Pirmin assure me that everything looked right?" He did not expect anything like this.

Everyone else there was well aware of the death. They were not surprised at hearing it mentioned. On the contrary, they were all eager to see when Garaidi would bring it up. Nevertheless, they were concerned. How were those two going to react? Would they become angry? Would they begin making excuses? No one knew!

"At that time," said Garaidi confidently, "they all said that she died of typhus. It was a lie! Muñube's uncle could shed some light on this if he were alive today."

"My uncle's name is out," thought Muñube, "Of course, Garaidi had to mention it sooner or later! But, how did he help Egurmendi? How?"

"And do you know why they lied?" asked Garaidi without pause, looking at all of them in turn. "They had to find a reason to bury her immediately, and they came up with the excuse of a contagious disease so no one would see the gunshot wound in her forehead. And . . . with the assistance of the late Dr. Muñube, everything worked out seamlessly . . . Until today, that is."

Pirmin was ready to explode and so was Egurmendi, whose usual calm demeanor had transformed into obvious anxiety. What happened to his composure? What about his esteemed reputation? After hearing all that had been said, how could he keep holding his head high?

Garaidi intentionally paused once more to

make sure that what he had just said had been clearly understood. But no one said a word.

"That woman," he continued, "had just arrived from Belgium and, if I'm not mistaken, few in town had seen her. Among you, other than Mr. Egurmendi, only Mr. Elurzabal had seen her. Here's her photograph."

It was the same photograph they saw at Egurmendi's house. Somehow, he must have gotten a hold of it. He approached Muñube and asked him: "Do you recognize her?"

Wide eyed and in a faint voice, he replied:

"She looks like Begoña!"

"You said it yourself. She looks like Begoña, Pagodi's daughter, your girlfriend. Are you surprised that the woman in the photograph resembles Begoña? Well, don't be. That's her mother!"

But, what was he saying? Begoña was Pagodi's daughter and the daughter of Egurmendi's wife? How could that be? What happened between Pagodi and Egurmendi? Had Pagodi run away because of whatever their dealings had been? Did he run away with Egurmendi's wife of all people? But didn't that woman die the same day Pagodi 'disappeared'? Wasn't Begoña born later? What kind of mess was this? It was ridiculous! Had he lost his mind? Was he joking?

As bewildering as it seemed, as Garaidi kept talking, Egurmendi grew calmer. Were they both out of their minds? Where they teasing the others?

"Yes, gentlemen," said Garaidi, not worried a bit about what the others might have been thinking. He couldn't have cared less. "Yes, gentlemen. Begoña, Muñube's girlfriend, is the daughter of Pagodi and the woman whom you all thought was Egurmendi's wife. But now, before you reach unfounded conclusions, I must clarify something else. That woman . . . was never Egurmendi's wife. Egurmendi is single, not a widower. That woman was Pagodi's wife. Would you like to explain what happened yourself?" he asked Egurmendi who, by then, had given up and was considering whether to chime in or not.

Egurmendi shifted in his chair, cleared his throat and now, with everyone's undivided attention, began slowly explaining what happened all those years back, everything he had kept, bottled up, inside for so long.

"Many years ago,"

30

# Conclusion

". . . when Pagodi and I were in Belgium . . . ," Egurmendi began, ". . . he happened to fall in love with a young Belgian woman and planned to marry her. It was about then when that dreadful war broke out. Unexpectedly, in a matter of a few days, German troops entered the village and engaged in tremendous battles with the French. Fire, machine gun bursts, explosions everywhere. One of those horrific days, Pagodi's fiancée, after finishing her workday, headed home to find it destroyed and burned to the ground. Her parents and two brothers perished there and, that same day, the Germans arrested and imprisoned her younger sister because all in the family clandestinely opposed the Germans. She was left alone, inconsolable; she came to us, asking for help. What could we do in such a situation? We thought hard and finally decided that Pagodi and Mari should get married as soon as possible and that the three of us should return here. But it was easier said than done. Even though Pagodi and I were foreigners and hadn't taken sides in the war, it wasn't easy to move around freely; you had to obtain the Germans' permission. It was impossible for Mari to obtain travel documents, which meant that we had to hide, be on the run, with the Germans after her. Those were terrible days, terrifying days. Once, while we were on the run, the Germans showed up suddenly, looking for us at the inn where we were hiding. There must've been a spy around. In utter distress, we somehow slipped out through a back door. Mari and I were able to hide but they caught Pagodi. Finally, the two of us, some way or other, made it to the Swiss border. I pretended to be a foreign student and, so she could escape with me, we said that Mari was my wife. We lied and said that we were newlyweds and that we lost all our identification documents in the battle of Liege. The border guards skeptically questioned our story but finally allowed us, the Egurmendi husband and wife, as they said, to pass. Once we were safe in Switzerland, we learned that Pagodi had been arrested, accused of being a spy and of conspiring with Mari against them. Mari had been an active member of the resistance. Since we were free in Switzerland, we decided that for, Pagodi and Mari's sister's sake, we would keep pretending to be married. We acted as husband and wife there and when we came here . . . we continued the charade. As soon as we could, we called Pagodi's father and we all began working together to bring his son back and, a few days later, he was here, among us. After that . . . Mr. Garaidi already told you what happened. Other than that . . . well . . ."

"That's more or less what I have found out, too," began Garaidi, seeing that Egurmendi was losing steam. "Surely you are wondering why all this wasn't explained openly at the time. Well, have you all forgotten the woman who lies buried in the Egurmendi-family mausoleum, killed by a gunshot?"

True! Everyone was openmouthed, listening to Egurmendi's account, and had forgotten. Even Txomin, distracted by the latest developments, had forgotten about the corpse he himself discovered. He felt anew the terror he suffered at the time of the discovery.

After glancing at his watch, Garaidi continued swiftly:

"Let's keep undoing this knot and pull another thread. I don't want to go on and on for too long, because there's someone waiting for us. Last week, I went to Zugarramurdi, a small village right on the French border. This village has a beautiful church and only three streets, one that goes up, one that goes down and a third one . . . that lies flat. Mr. Pirmin Elurzabal is very familiar with Zugarramurdi because he's from there.

Many villagers work as smugglers, moving all kinds of illegal goods from one side of the border to the other. The Elurzabals knew about this type of operation because they were smugglers, too. But let's get back to the point. One night, like many during the time of all the events we've been discussing, the Elurzabals were bringing a very precious cargo across the border from France. That dark night ended up being a very sorrowful one for the Elurzabal family. As they neared their house, suddenly, down by the creek, they stumbled upon some riflemen, border guards. They dropped their cargo carelessly and fled for their lives, running from hill to hill with the authorities right on their heels, shooting at them. Unfortunately, it looks like Elurzabal's sister was in the area, probably trying to help, when, unexpectedly . . . she was shot in the head and fell face down. Her brother, running next to her, did his best to hoist her to his shoulder and keep running.

Hiding here and there, one of them half-dead, the other one like a rabbit on the run, they barely escaped. Thankfully, the border guards did not recognize the smugglers. Otherwise . . . Finally, they took their sister home. But, how could they explain their sister's condition without giving up information about their whereabouts that night? Her wound was no scratch. She was unconscious, but still alive, and they had to do something quickly, so they called their brother, a servant at Egurmendi's house in Urgain. I'm not sure how but, that very morning, they took her there, to Egurmendi's home. Once there, they called Muñube, the old doctor, an excellent physician and a very close friend of the Egurmendis. Doctor Muñube did all he could but wasn't able to save her. With Mr. Elurzabal's help, accompanied by his fiancé, Mari, Pagodi headed for France. Pagodi 'disappeared' on the same day the woman died. Of course, it was her body that was buried as that of Egurmendi's wife."

He paused for a moment and then continued:

"Why did they spin such an elaborate yarn?" he asked while his audience listened in awe. "Well, on one hand, Egurmendi didn't have to explain publicly that his wedding was a sham. If people would have known, wouldn't the town have been abuzz? What a topic for the gossips. One the other hand, Pagodi and Mari could get married right away. Also, when the news of 'Mari's' death reached German ears, they would stop pressuring Mari's sister to inform on her. She would finally be left alone. And lastly, the Elurzabal family wouldn't have to confess that they were the smugglers on that ill-fated night. And good or bad, right or wrong, that is what they did."

Everyone smiled relieved. Garaidi stood and concluded with these words:

"Gentlemen! We, the eight of us, are the only ones who know the truth of these events. Many of you actually, all of you were mistaken. Some believed that Egurmendi was a cruel assassin, others accused Elurzabal, and still others believed it had been Muñube. It appears, however, that all are innocent of any wrongdoing. And yet, you were so sure! I must admit that, when we found out about the body in the Egurmendi gravesite, all of us, starting with myself, began suspecting people. And we thought we knew who the killer was. It is second nature for men to look for a scapegoat, to suspect the worst, to hang the blame on someone. There's an old saying from somewhere that goes: 'if you think wrong of someone you will have guessed right.' It looks like we have been working hard to make this saying true among us. We know that all that glitters is not gold, but how often do we forget that all that smells bad is not manure? That is why I have asked all of you to come. What would be the consequences if we had spread our suspicions in the village before we learned the truth? What if our suspicions had turned into gossip on the street? It is easy to pull a nail from a piece of wood, but what about the hole it leaves behind? A hole stays a hole! If we sullied the good name of a decent man by spreading these whispers and murmurs, no matter how hard we tried, it would be difficult to prove his decency, and just as the hole stays a hole, some mean-spirited, scandal-mongering coward would perpetuate the slander now or later, here or there, the what ifs and maybes. A fire, whatever its size still burns. For this reason, to keep anything like that from happening here and to preserve everyone's good name, I ask that you kindly keep all you have learned today a secret. That's all."

They praised Garaidi with one voice.

Amunda, walked up to Egurmendi and, with eyes shining, holding back tears, said:

"Forgive me for suspecting you, my daughter will be so happy . . ."

Herriburu also approached and stretched out his hand.

"I'm happy old friend," he said, eagerly.

Muñube too, feeling his deep animosity fade in realization of all Egurmendi had done for Begoña's parents, came up and offered his thanks.

For his part, Txomin smiled and scratched the back of his ear, happy and relieved that everything ended well. It goes without saying that Egurmendi and Pirmin Elurzabal were ecstatic.

Meanwhile, Garaidi called for his maid by ringing the bell that rested on the table. When she opened the door (hadn't he just said that the door was locked?):

"Has the woman arrived?" he asked her.

"Yes, she arrived a while ago."

"Take these two gentlemen to her, then."

Addressing Egurmendi and Muñube:

"Go to see Begoña first. She's in the next room. Karmentxo will join you right away."

And to Amunda:

"Go to the dining room, fetch your daughter and take her to Egurmendi so their heartache ends and they renew their love. And the rest of you . . . have a drink with me."

A half-hour later, they were all together, deep in conversation, when the maid showed up; a little put-off and looking at Garaidi, she said:

"An old man who doesn't shut up came a while ago saying that he must see you . . ."

"I bet it's Joxe Jokin," Garaidi told his wife under his breath, laughing.

"I bet it is."

"Who does he say he is?" Garaidi asked his maid.

"Joxe Jokin, from Urgain."

"Let him in, let him in!" Garaidi said and then, quietly, to everyone else:

"Make sure you don't tell him anything about this! Not a word!"

"Here he is," said the maid while ushering Joxe Jokin to the room.

"There is no way my daughter would hire you as a maid. What a grouch!" said Joxe Jokin, about to walk into the room, sounding like a bugle, loud enough for all gathered to hear.

"If she's as talkative as you, I wouldn't want to work for her, either!"

"My daughter, talkative?" Joxe Jokin grumbled, in a bad mood. "My daughter, talkative?

Why should my daughter be talkative? Was your mother a fool?"

One point for Joxe Jokin!

We're not sure if the maid understood Joxe Jokin's jab, but more than one of the guests burst into laughter. They were howling when Joxe Jokin finally entered the room.

"Hey! What's going on here? What corn husking happened here?"

www.ingramcontent.com/pod-product-compliance
Lightning Source LLC
LaVergne TN
LVHW090935080826
845145LV00003B/759

* 9 7 8 1 9 3 5 7 0 9 5 7 2 *